# Trapped

## FEARLESS
### BOOK THREE

ANNIE JOCOBY

# Chapter One

Dalilah had just called me, and, once again, I started to feel apprehensive. I hated that she just said those words again – that we need to talk. The last time she said something like that to me, she dumped me. At any rate, those words sounded just ominous to me.

"Okay, Dalilah, are you coming home, or would you like to meet me somewhere?"

"I'm in the city," she said. "Could you meet me on the corner of 5th and Park? I'm in a *Starbucks* here. I'm so sorry, I would like to come home, but I need to stay in the city, too. There's something that I need to do, and I need you by my side to do it."

That sounded more encouraging to me. That she needed me by her side, as opposed to something else. I relaxed a little bit. "Okay, I'll be there. Just give me about an hour or so. I'll see you in a bit."

"Luke?"

"Yes?"

"I love you. I really, really do." At that, she started to cry softly, and I got concerned. What was going on? Did she see a doctor without telling me? Was she really sick?

"I love you too. I'll see you in a few."

I shook my head as I got into the shower and got dressed. It was my dream that we had made it through our traumas, and came out the other side. But did we? Was there something else, something worse than ever, which greeted us? I couldn't imagine what that would be, but Dalilah wasn't the kind of person who would just start crying for no reason at all.

My apprehension grew as I boarded the subway to make it to Fifth and Park. My heart was in my throat, absolutely. I didn't know why it seemed that happiness was always in reach, yet always so very far away. Too far away, it seemed. It was like the Greek myth about Tantalus – the fruit was always just beyond his reach, and the water was just beyond his mouth to drink. That was his fate. That was his punishment. It seemed appropriate, because I had felt like Tantalus since the day that I met Dalilah.

Happiness was just around the corner, until it wasn't.

When I got to the *Starbucks*, and saw Dalilah's tear-stained face, I knew. I knew that happiness was just out of reach, once more.

"What is it, Dalilah?" I asked, sitting down next to her. I took her hand and kissed it, and then kissed her forehead. "Please don't tell me that you're really sick." God forbid. Maybe she had a terminal disease. I tried to put that thought out of my mind, but it still crept into my brain until it became something that I simply couldn't shake.

She shook her head, but just cried more. Finally, after a few minutes, she just said "I don't know what to say. How to say this. I just don't know."

"That's okay," I said. "You can tell me when you're ready."

She cried for a few minutes, and then took a deep breath. "Okay," she said. "Before I tell you what I need to tell you, I first have to give you a kind of dry lecture on New York family law. I know that this is going to seem out of place, but you need to know this so that you can know that what I have to do is something that is absolutely necessary. I've tried to think my way around this, but nothing is coming to me just yet."

I relaxed a little bit. It sounded like she wasn't, in fact, going to tell me that she had a terminal disease or a severe sickness. I nodded my head. "Okay, go on with the dry lecture," I said with a smile.

Another deep breath from her. "So," she began. "There's this concept in New York law, and most any state law, really, called putative father. That means if there is a child conceived during a marriage, that child is presumed to be the child of the husband in that marriage."

My heart started to quicken. I suddenly knew exactly where she was going with this, and all of her sickness in the past week or so was starting to make sense. Still, I didn't interrupt. She obviously had to tell me everything, and I was going to let her.

She nodded her head. "There's also a standard used by judges known as the best interest of the child. That means that a judge has discretion on anything legal that involves the child. There are no hard and fast rules when it comes to issues such as child custody and whether to allow DNA evidence or a paternity action during a divorce proceeding."

I took a deep breath. "Dalilah, I know where you're going with this," I said. I suddenly felt like jumping for joy that she was pregnant, hopefully with my baby. But that feeling was tempered by the sobering thought that the baby might not be mine at all, and that Dalilah apparently was none too happy about it. I knew why- from what she was telling me, it sounded like Nottingham would have rights to the child, no matter who was the actual father. Just because he blackmailed her into marrying him.

She started crying harder. "Yes, Luke, I'm pregnant. I'm not sure how far along I am. Not very, because the home pregnancy test I took just recently indicated pregnancy. But I am pregnant. I know that it's yours, Luke. I can feel it in my gut."

"I don't understand," I said. "How can that be? You started to feel nauseated right after you and I made love. Don't those symptoms come on later?" My heart started sinking. Perhaps the baby wasn't mine at all.

"Yes, usually," she said. "But sometimes women start feeling it right away. Nobody can explain why, but sometimes it just starts really early. Within a couple of days."

I wasn't convinced. I understood that Dalilah had sex with Nottingham. She had explained that to me when she and I got back together – that she felt that she needed to submit to keep him happy. Another sacrifice that she made for me, and that was the worst one of all, she said.

How could she really know who was the father in this situation?

"Okay," I said. "Now, calm down. We'll get through this. No matter what, I'm not running. We'll get through this together."

Even as I said those words, though, I wasn't convinced. I knew as well as she that the child would be Nottingham's, no matter what, and that Nottingham would screw up that child royally.

She shook her head. "Oh, Luke, you don't know the things that I know. The children of men like him – they're awful. No morals, entitled. Not to mention the fact that he's abusive. What kind of a chance would my child have with that kind of an influence in his or her life? I would be bringing in a child that would have little chance of living a normal and happy life. I mean, I will provide as much guidance and love as I can, as will you, I know, but I will only be half of the equation. I just don't see how it can work."

I got up abruptly and started to pace. Dalilah helped me out of my jams, so now it was time for me to do the same. "Okay," I said, "let's brainstorm this." That was my first instinct. I didn't want to look at the situation emotionally, because if I did, I knew that I would demand that she keep the child. Because I knew in my own gut that the baby would really be mine. "Is there any way that a judge will allow a DNA test to prove who is really the father?"

Dalilah nodded her head. "I saw an attorney today. She said that it would entirely depend on what judge we get. Some judges will allow it, others won't. Unfortunately for us, Nottingham is friendly with most of those judges, which complicates matters further."

"But you and I can still do a DNA test to show that I'm the dad, right? I mean, there's nothing stopping us from doing that, right?"

"Of course," she said. "We can do a private DNA test, but whether or not it's allowed in court is another matter. And, even if it is allowed in court, whether or not a judge will actually sever Nottingham's rights is still another matter." She shook her head. "It's all so complicated."

"So," he said. "A judge doesn't allow it, and we appeal that decision. What about that?"

"Appeals courts won't overturn a decision unless it was some kind of gross error. Gross error means that no reasonable judge would make the decision that the trial court judge made, given the facts and circumstances. In this case, there's no way that an appeals court will strike down the trial court if they deny the request to admit the DNA evidence. Nottingham and I were still together under the same roof right before this baby came into being. It would be entirely reasonable for a judge to decide not to disturb Nottingham's rights to the child."

I shook my head. Dalilah had done her homework, of course. "Sounds like you've been reading up."

"I did look at case law," she said. "Of course."

I put my hands behind my neck and lowered my head. "Dalilah," I said. "I can understand the predicament that you're in. I really can. And, if it weren't for this whole Nottingham situation, I'd be over the moon with joy. I know that we're young, but I'd love to have a child with you." I didn't express the fear that I couldn't really provide for the child. I knew that I had to use the fact that a baby was on the way to work harder than ever to get a foothold in the art scene. I would be a great provider for both Dalilah and the baby, I just knew it.

"Well," Dalilah said. "I would be overjoyed, too, Luke. It's my dream to have a beautiful baby with you. But that's not the situation that we're looking at. The odds are long that Nottingham won't have at least split custody with this baby, and I can't bring a child into the world knowing that Nottingham is going to have a chance to make the child's life hell. Not to mention the fact that his hatred for me would probably cause him to take all of that out on the baby. How can I bring a baby into the world knowing all of this?"

I paced the floor. "Dalilah, please. Don't make a hasty decision. You just have to have faith that it will all work out fine. We'll find a judge who will allow DNA evidence and will be willing to sever Nottingham's parental rights. Or we'll prove that Nottingham will be an unfit father, which will give you all the rights. Something can be done, Dalilah. You just have to believe that it will all work out in the end."

"Luke, don't be naïve," she said. "Nottingham's attorney, according to the attorney I saw this morning, is an aggressive shark. Don't even think that we can prevail in a custody action if the judge refuses to allow DNA evidence. It won't happen. I'll be lucky if Nottingham doesn't end up with sole custody, as soon as everything is said and done."

I bit my lip. "There's a way out of this, Dalilah. There has to be. I mean, if this is my kid, I don't think that..." I shook my head, as the enormity of what was about to happen came down on me. Dalilah maybe was carrying my child, and she wanted to kill him or her. I fought back tears. "Do you believe in something, Daliah? Something larger than us?"

Dalilah took a deep breath. "I don't know," she said. "Intellectually, I don't. Emotionally, I'd like to believe that this world is not all there is."

"But nobody really knows," I said. "Is that safe to say?"

"Of course. Everybody thinks that they know, but nobody really does."

"So, what happens to this baby? Does this baby just lose his or her only chance to live? Or do you think that maybe the spirit will just go on and have a chance with somebody else?"

"Luke, I know what you're saying," she said. "I've actually had the same questions myself. Which is why this decision is far from easy."

"But what if it is this life is this child's only chance? Maybe he or she will be the next Beethoven or Madame Curie."

"Or the next Ted Bundy or Hitler," Dalilah said. "I'm not persuaded by that argument."

"Okay," he said. "But think about all the children who came into this world unwanted. Some of them have gone on to do great things. And there are plenty of children who aren't necessarily great, but the parents can't imagine life without them. Children aren't always convenient, Dalilah. They're often a surprise. But the parents usually love them anyhow, and are so grateful that they didn't terminate them when they had the chance."

"I understand all of that," she said. "But this is a unique situation, don't you think? In this case, there won't be two loving parents bringing the child up. There will be one loving one and one abusive monster involved. The chance that this child is going to grow up being completely messed up is exponentially more than with children who come into the world with two sane people as parents."

"But what if it's mine?" I said. "I think that it is. I know that I also have a gut feeling that I'm the dad. When you told me that you were pregnant, I just had the feeling that you were carrying my child. I don't want....I really don't want my child to die."

Dalilah, all at once, started to look angry. "I know that, Luke. Don't you think I know that? I want this child so much. I really do. If I weren't married to Nottingham, it would be a welcome thing. Even though we're young, and neither of us have much money, I still would want this baby with you. But that's not the situation here."

I sat down, and took her hands. I looked into her eyes. "Dalilah, I'm not a religious person at all. I don't know what I believe. I think that I do believe in something. Not sure what. But I do believe in fate and faith. You have to have faith that this will all work out for us in the end. Something will happen that will ensure that Nottingham won't get his depraved hands on this baby. It's going to be stressful, and it's going to be hell, but it will work out in the end. But if you terminate now, there's no chance for it working out in the end. And you might deprive both of us of something really wonderful."

Dalilah started to shake her head. "Luke, please. I don't want this to come between us."

"How can it not? Even if the baby is legally his, it might actually be mine. How can this situation not come between us?"

"What if I'm pressured into having the baby, and everything that I predict comes true? Nottingham gets custody, and proceeds to make the child's life hell. I'll be dealing with that for the rest of my life. Won't that come between us, too? You're going to resent me for terminating, but I might resent you for talking me out of it."

I sat down, and put my head in my hands. Another impossible situation we were in. Damned if we did, and damned if we didn't.

I wished so much that I had a crystal ball that would tell me how all of this was going to shake out. She was absolutely right – there was a chance that this baby was going to cause an interminable amount of grief. I foresaw a heated custody battle, and Nottingham doing his best to screw up the child. Dalilah was going to go through hell, and so would I. There probably would be no way around it.

So, I blurted out the first thing that came to my mind. "We run. We go and live in another country, and Nottingham won't find us. We change our names and our identities, and we run. That's what we do. That's what we do, Dalilah. We run."

To my surprise, Dalilah actually looked hopeful. "That could work," she said. "I have some Irish relatives. Distant ones, for sure, as they're the descendants of my grandma Maggie's cousins. At least one of those descendants is living in London as we speak. His name is Liam. I don't know much about him, but maybe my dad could get in touch with him and see if he could put us up for a spell. Just until we can get used to that city and find our way around it."

I nodded my head. London actually sounded like an awesome idea to me. The art scene there was thriving, especially for my kind of cutting edge works, and Dalilah's, too. And Paris was just a train ride away. "London," I said. "I love that idea. But what if Nottingham tracks us down there? I was actually thinking of something more like Siberia or Bora Bora." I was only half-joking, really. London sounded like a heavenly idea, but it wasn't exactly the most inauspicious place. Nottingham Industries was international, which meant that Nottingham would be doing business in London. The chances of us running into him would be slight, but still a problem. And if he runs into us and sees that there's a child...I shuddered to think such a thing.

"No, Luke," she said. "We'll just have to do a good job of covering our tracks. Living like two people in the witness protection plan. I don't quite know how we're going to be able to change our identities, but perhaps that won't even be a problem. London is a big place, Luke. We could get lost in there. Nottingham won't know to look there for us, either. And, best of all, we'd both have a fresh start with our art. I'll be sad to leave my family, of course, but Nick owns a house in Italy, and my dad has a winery there, too. They go to Europe all the time. We'll still be able to see them."

Was this going to work? It didn't matter, it had to be done. Even if it didn't work, we had to at least try. It was a plan, which was better than the other plans that we managed to cook up. It was infinitely better than terminating the child, and also infinitely better than letting the child be ruined by Nottingham. Of that, I was sure.

Of everything else, I was less sure.

# Chapter Two

## DALILAH

So, we were going to run. Was it the ideal situation? Hell, no. The ideal situation would be that there wasn't a baby at all. But it did seem to be the best solution, considering the circumstances.

I really didn't see any way around it. That I would be charged with possible kidnapping if Nottingham ever found out about the baby and the fact that I ran to keep it from him, was not even on my radar. Luke and I were going to have to take a chance that we would never be found.

But, deep down, I knew that it was fruitless. Nottingham was going to track me down. If he had to send private investigators to every part of the globe, he was going to do it. Even if he didn't know about the baby.

I had to try, though. At the very least, I had to give Luke and me some distance from the whole Nottingham situation, so that I could think about my next move. There was a way out of this, I knew it, that didn't necessarily involve Luke and I running from place to place for the rest of our lives, like fugitives. I just didn't see it, but it would come to me.

In the meantime, though, I had to tell my mom and dad about all of this mess. Like it or not, I was going to have to tell them. If nothing else, dad might be able to contact Liam and see if I could stay with him. I didn't know much about Liam, except that he was some kind of mogul over in London, and was very wealthy. He was young, only 27, and had made a fortune in the music business, representing some of the hottest acts in the world, before establishing his own record label. Last I knew, he was literally a self-made billionaire.

I personally had never met the guy, which made it strange that I was going to try to see if I could stay with him for the time being. But he was the only relative that I knew who lived in London. All the other Gallaghers were scattered around Cork, Drogheda and Dublin. As much as I had always wanted to live in Ireland, secretly, I knew that London had a much hotter art scene. This would give both of us a fresh start, which Luke was desperately needing after the apparent rejection from all of the people he met at his premiere. I looked forward to getting a fresh start, myself.

So, a few days after Luke and I had made our tentative plans to run away from the whole Nottingham situation, I found myself waiting for my mom, dad, Nick and Scotty to meet me for dinner at Wolfgang Puck's. I dreaded talking to them, but I asked Nick to at least give mom and dad a heads-up on the topic of discussion that day. Mom had already called me, hysterical at the thought that I was thinking of terminating my child. I had to talk her down off the ledge, but I managed to get it under control when I reassured her that I wouldn't be depriving her of a grandchild after all.

They met me, and we all sat down.

"Okay," I said, addressing the four people at the table. The four people who, aside from Luke, meant the absolute most to me in the world. "I guess Nick has filled all of you in on the fact that I'm pregnant, and what that means, considering my situation with Nottingham."

"Yes," my dad said. "I've already gotten in touch with some of the best family law attorneys in the city. I've gotten a few lined up that will help you fight this one all the way."

I shook my head. "You'll be fighting fire with fire. Whoever you find to represent me, Nottingham will have better. You aren't the only billionaire involved in this situation, dad. You can't throw money at this and hope that it resolves itself."

"I don't understand," mom said. "You assured me that you would keep this child. And you don't seem to want to fight Nottingham in court. So, what is your plan?"

I took a deep breath. "My plan is to move to London and start fresh. Luke and I have already talked it through, and we know the possible consequences."

My dad was shaking his head. "No, you can't do that. That is essentially kidnapping, I hope you know that. You're going to be acting like a criminal by doing that, and you will also be treated like a criminal when Nottingham finds out what happened. You have to face this. I didn't fight enough when I found out that you were going to marry that man, but I'm putting my foot down now. You can't do this."

I sighed. I was prepared for this. "Dad, once again, it's not a matter of my asking permission. I'm an adult. You can't stop me. And believe me, I've thought about this situation eight ways to Sunday. I see no other solution. Yes, there could be devastating consequences if Nottingham sees what I've done, but I'll just have to face them if it comes to that. The other solutions to this situation are untenable. Either I terminate or I let Nottingham ruin this baby. Neither of those are options for me. I mean, I admit, the first idea I had was to have an abortion. But Luke made me see that there was possibly another way. And I'm going to take it. The odds are against us living our lives in peace, but I like the odds of Luke and I getting away with this a helluva lot more than the odds that Nottingham won't get custody of this child."

Dad was still shaking his head. "I won't see my daughter become a criminal."

I took a deep breath, and looked at Nick, who, surprisingly enough, wasn't saying a word.

I raised an eyebrow. "Sometimes, dad, you have to break the law if a situation is bad enough. I would think that you, of all people, would know this." I looked at Nick again, pointedly, and he shook his head.

Dad looked over at Nick, and then back at me. "How did you know?"

"I just do," I said. "I was a bratty kid, and wanting to learn how to do subversive things. I taught myself to hack, and I found out about Paul Lucas, and what really happened to him. And all that I can say is that Uncle Nick is in no position to..."

Scotty's face got white, and I immediately felt bad. Nick looked like he was going to come over to my side of the table and strangle me with his bare hands. He turned to Scotty. "Scotty, honey, I need to speak with Dalilah alone."

Scotty just put her hand on his, and said "no need. I know. I've always known what happened to that bastard. I've just never told you that I knew."

I immediately felt terrible for bringing up this can of worms, especially since that was apparently some kind of secret between Nick and Scotty all of these years.

"Crap," Nick said. "Then I guess I need to talk to you alone. Later, though." He shook his head and addressed me. "When are you going to stop bringing this up, Dalilah? It happened, it was years ago, and he got what was coming to him. Let it go."

It was my dad's turn to look mystified. "Wait," he said to Nick. "You knew that Dalilah found out about that, and you never told me?"

He shrugged. "I didn't find it to have any relevance. Dalilah promised, on her word, that she wouldn't let that whole sorry incident out of the bag, but, apparently, she's not good with her word."

"Listen," I said. "I only brought that up to let you guys know that sometimes you have to make solutions that are not exactly legal, when you're up against the wall. That's what I'm going to do, here."

Dad looked like he wanted to slap me, which is a look that I had never seen on his face. "Two wrongs don't make a right," he said. "Listen, I've made mistakes in my life. Nick has, too. Your mother has made mistake, Scotty too. We've all made mistakes. Some of them were pretty huge ones. But that doesn't give you *carte blanche* to repeat the pattern."

"That wasn't a mistake, Ryan," Nick said. "Paul Lucas wasn't a mistake. He got what was coming to him, and you know it."

"That's not the topic of conversation, here," dad said to Nick. "The topic is whether or not my daughter will commit a felony by doing what she's planning on doing. Dalilah is the topic, here, not what you and I did 17 years ago to a pervert who didn't really deserve to live."

"Huh, dad," I said. "Nick made himself judge, jury and executioner of that man. And you're going to lecture me on what I'm about to do?"

At that, my dad slapped my face, hard. I put my hand up to my cheek, and looked at him. He had an expression that I had never seen in my entire life. His face was red, his eyes menacing, his mouth turned down. "You will never talk to me like that again," he said. "How did you turn out like this? So devious, so underhanded. I didn't raise you to be a criminal. And you will never bring up Nick's past to try to justify your shitty actions. You will face up to what you wrought by doing what you did with Nottingham – using him, getting trapped by him, and marrying him for the wrong reasons – and you will do it within the bounds of the law. Do I make myself clear?"

"Crystal," I said, thinking to myself that I was just going to have to run away with Luke without his blessing. I looked over at my mother, who wasn't saying much. She at least seemed to have a little bit of humility, considering all the devious things that she did in her own youth. Namely, running away from my dad when she was pregnant with me. She, essentially, did what I was proposing to do in this situation, only my motivation for doing so was much, much different than her motivations for running away all those years ago.

Ironic. For once, my mom really seemed to understand me. At least, if I read her expression correctly, she understood me. It seemed that she was furtively trying to give her non-verbal approval for what it was that I was going to do.

My mom put her hand on my dad's. "Calm down, Ryan," she said. "Listen, you and I have to talk about this later."

"There's nothing to talk about," dad said. "I know what you're thinking, beautiful, and it's not the same thing at all. You running from me when you were pregnant with Dalilah wasn't the same thing as what Dalilah is proposing to do."

"It's not?" mom asked. "What's the difference?"

"For one, you knew that I wouldn't press charges for kidnapping. At least, I hope that you knew that."

"Regardless, it's the same thing," mom counteracted. "If you're going to call Dalilah a felon, then you're essentially saying that I'm a felon, too. Really, if you get to the heart of the matter, that's true."

Oh, god. Now, I was turning everybody against each other. I never wanted to drive a wedge between my parents, let alone Nick and Scotty, yet it seemed that everybody was angry with one another all of a sudden.

13

I dug up their pasts in a way that I probably shouldn't have. I essentially opened the long-festering sores that lay deep underneath two seemingly rock-solid marriages. I immediately tried to put a lid on it, while telling them that I was still going to run, and they couldn't stop me anymore than they could have stopped me from marrying that bastard in the first place.

I put my hands in the "time-out" position. "Listen, let's focus, here. I'm really sorry that I'm bringing up sore subjects. I never meant for this meeting to result in there being hard feelings between all of you. But I also want to let you guys know that you should empathize with my situation. You guys have been in impossible situations before, and you took care of it how you saw fit."

I looked at my mother, and took her hand. "Mom, you ran from dad when you were pregnant with me. I understand why, too, considering that whole Natalie mess. Dad forgave you, and you two moved on."

Then I looked at Nick. "You plotted the death of the man who was doing horrible things to Aunt Scotty. I'm quite sure that you didn't want to do that, but you did. You did, because you understood that doing that was the only real solution to an impossible knot of a problem."

My father shook his head. "What kind of an example have I set for my own daughter?" He no longer looked angry, but, instead, looked extremely sad. "Dalilah, please understand. Everybody at this table has done terrible things. With the possible exception of Scotty. But, please don't repeat the pattern. I know it sounds hypocritical and like I'm telling you to do as I say, not as I do."

I felt sorry for him, because he looked so defeated. I saw in his face that he was beginning to understand that nothing that he could say or do would stop me from doing what it was that I felt was necessary. I also saw in his expression the shame and guilt over his own actions in the past, and the apparent effect that these actions had on me. He knew that he had little moral ground to stand on in lecturing me, and this devastated him beyond measure. I knew that, just by reading his facial expression and body language.

Of course, I had no idea exactly what role my dad played in the Paul

Lucas affair. I did know that he at least knew about it, and probably approved of it. This made him as guilty as Nick in my book. This would be why he was coming across as so guilty.

"Dad, don't blame yourself," I said. "Truth be told, I've always at least tried to be a good girl. I haven't succeeded by any stretch of the imagination. I keep getting myself into these impossible knots, and, when it comes to this one, I see no way out of it except for to try to run from it. If you can tell me a truly viable solution to my problem, I'm all ears. And, no, telling me that we're going to fight Nottingham in court isn't a viable solution to me. Because you and I both know that the chances of prevailing on this will be slim at best."

Dad just looked at me with those sad green eyes. I felt depressed just seeing that expression on his face. So much regret, guilt and shame in those eyes...my mom had a similar expression, but hers was more sadness for knowing that I, once again, had screwed up my life. And that I, once again, was about to do something to possibly screw it up even further.

Finally, dad just sighed. "What's your plan?"

"Well, I was wondering if you could contact Liam Gallagher for me. I know that you're not close with him, and you barely know him, but he's the only person I can think of who lives in London. I know that he has a palatial mansion, too, and I hope that he might take in two vagabonds who have no place to go."

"And then what?" dad asked. "What are you going to do once you're over there?"

"Try to make it in the London art scene. Luke and I both are eager to re-start our art careers. London would be the perfect place to do it. And, while we're there, we'll be thinking of ways to get around the whole Nottingham thing. I know that there's an underlying solution to this whole thing, that will involve both of us eventually returning to New York with our heads held high, but I just don't know what that solution would be just yet."

Dad shook his head. "Oh, god, is there any way that I can talk you out of this?"

"No," I said. "I'm doing it, with your help or without. Luke and I are both pretty broke, although he does have some money saved up from the proceeds from his show. That money will go fast, though, in an expensive city such as London. I would love to have a place to stay while we both try to get established. So, please, dad, please could you talk to grandma Maggie about talking to Liam? I know that she's in touch with her cousins, so it probably would be best to be coming from her."

Dad shook his head, defeated. His shoulders were slumped, and his head was down.

"Okay," he finally said. "I'll do what I can."

# Chapter Three

O n the way home from dinner, I drove to my house with my wife by my side. She wasn't saying a word. But her eyes conveyed to me that she was in as much pain as I was about this whole mess. If that was even possible, because I felt that I couldn't feel much lower than I did right at that moment.

I reached over for her hand, and she took it and gave me a weak smile. "I know what you're thinking, and none of this is your fault. Or mine, for that matter. We've always known that she was going to be handful. Right from the very start. I still remember the first time that I knew that she was special. She said a word when she was just four months old, and knew what it meant. I knew, right then and there, that she was going to give us trouble."

I sighed. "I know, beautiful. I know it's not our fault. But it doesn't make any of this any easier. What's going to happen when Nottingham inevitably finds out what's going on? Then what? Our daughter will be lucky if she doesn't wind up serving time in prison, that's what. But how do we stop her? Aside from chaining her up in our basement, that is." I shook my head. "The sad thing is, she's almost right. There's very little that she can do in this situation that will have a good outcome. Of course, when Nottingham finds her and slaps her with felony kidnapping charges, he's going to be the sole custodian of that child."

Iris shook her head, tears in her eyes. "What can be done, here? I mean, within the bounds of the law, that is. We shoot the dice and hope that we get an understanding judge who will terminate Nottingham's rights? I just don't see that happening."

She took a deep breath. I knew what was next. "Tell me about Paul Lucas."

I shook my head. "I never wanted you to find out about that. But I know that you know the story of what he was doing to Scotty."

"I do. I remember."

"Well, Nick was at the end of his rope with that one. He was a complete waste of breath, that Paul Lucas, and he was threatening to completely make Scotty's life a living hell, even more than he already was. He threatened her, saying that she wouldn't be able to get a job in her field, and he unfortunately had the power to do just that. Make sure that she was a total pariah in the architecture world. And Nick had just had enough."

Iris nodded. "So, Nick forced him to commit suicide? He as good as murdered that man?"

"Yes. And I helped him plan it."

Iris got silent at that point. I took her hand, and rubbed it. "Talk to me, beautiful. What's on your mind?"

"I have mixed emotions about that, to be honest with you. I mean, I know that, sometimes, people literally don't deserve to live. If they're serial killers or serial rapists like that Paul Lucas, or something like that, the world is better off without them. But, at the same time, Dalilah was right. You and Nick were the judge, jury and executioner of that man. Is it any wonder that she won't listen to a word you say?"

"I never wanted that incident to be known. I never intended-"

"Yes, of course. You didn't intend for Dalilah to find out about it. Yet, she did. She did, and now she thinks that breaking the law is the right thing to do, as long as the outcome is beneficial to her. She can't get beyond that way of thinking, because her parents have not exactly shown her that there is a better way."

I knew that Iris was right about that, of course. As much as I wanted to bury, completely bury, what Nick and I had done all those years ago, I wasn't able to. And Dalilah now thought that my way was best, I guess.

The ends justify the means. I felt just like The Prince in Niccolo Machiavelli's novel about achieving ends with incredibly corrupt means. And the fact that I had passed this thinking down to my daughter devastated me beyond measure.

Iris squeezed my hand. "What's done is done. Anyhow, it probably doesn't really matter that you've done despicable things in your past. I think that Dalilah probably would have turned out just the same. And you know that she's going to do what she's going to do, no matter how much we lecture her against it. So, we might as well get in touch with Liam Gallagher, and ask if he'll take Dalilah and Luke in. If we don't, they'll end up running away to London without any visible means of support, and then god knows what will happen."

I shook my head. "That's kind of ridiculous, too, if you ask me. I mean, I could buy her a gorgeous flat over there, in a safe neighborhood. But you know that she wouldn't take it. She has never accepted my attempts to support her. Yet, she doesn't mind staying with a total stranger. She makes no sense to me, sometimes."

"Ah, but she's twenty. I don't think that you're supposed to make a lot of sense at that age, do you?"

"Touché. I just hope and pray that this whole thing doesn't blow up in everybody's face."

Iris sighed. "Even if it does, hopefully it will all turn out. I mean, look at all that blew up in our face when we first got together. And look at us now. It can work out."

I shook my head. "Yes, but we got lucky. You know we did. I should've died when Andrew shot me. One millimeter to the left or right, and I would have. I would have bled out before the ambulance got there. You should have died when Rochelle attacked you. And who the hell knows what would have happened had Nick not dragged you back from the West coast when you left me. I was so close to getting back to using, you can't even imagine. My will was dying a little bit every day. Everything worked out in the end, but it shouldn't have. It really shouldn't have."

"I know," Iris said. "I know. We made our share of mistakes. Especially me. Now it's our daughter's turn. I hate to be fatalistic about it all, and please don't think that I'm taking this all lightly, because I'm not.

But we really can't stop what she's going to do, so we just have to hope and pray that it will all turn out all right. And calling Liam and having him take in Dalilah and Luke will certainly be a step in the right direction."

"I know. Which is why I'm going to do just that. But not before I talk to my mother to make sure that Liam is an okay guy. I wish that we could go with her to check it all out, and make sure that she's not going from the frying pan into the fire. But I guess if my mother gives the go-ahead, that should be good enough."

That was really all I could do. Give Dalilah and safe place to land, and hope and pray that it all would work out.

# Chapter Four

## DALILAH

The past few days had been a whirlwind. Luke and I pretty much packed up our clothes, and he got the rest of his money out of the bank. Then we hightailed it out of New York City on my dad's private plane. I wasn't going to let my dad support me, still, but I wasn't totally stupid. Nor was I above borrowing his private plane for the journey across the pond.

From what I understood, Liam was willing to take us in. Even though he didn't know either of us from Adam. My father assured me that Liam was going to put out the welcome mat for Luke and me, and I was grateful for that. Just because we were kinda sorta family. Distant family, but family nonetheless.

We landed at Heathrow some seven hours after we departed. Both of us were jet-lagged and stressed. And I had been puking the entire way there, too. It was bad enough that I was pregnant, and feeling nauseated non-stop. The traveling didn't help matters at all.

I stepped out on the tarmac, and there was Liam, standing there with a sign that said "Dalilah" on it. He was a Gallagher, as far as looks go. The dark hair and the light eyes of my father and grandmother, and he was as tall as my dad, too. He was really a strikingly handsome guy, with his thick wavy hair and dimples, and it was also evident that, underneath the business suit he wore, he had a lean and muscular frame.

I squeezed Luke's hand, and he looked at me, concerned.

"Don't worry," I whispered. "He might be hot, but not as hot as you."

Luke shook his head. I could see worry on his face, and the worry was heightened as Liam looked at me appreciatively. Too appreciatively. He might be a cousin, but he was a distant cousin, so I suppose that his appreciative looks weren't too creepy.

"Hello, there, Dalilah Gallagher," he said, his handsome face lighting up. "Right happy to meet somebody from my dad's side of the family."

Luke went over the shake his hand, and Liam gripped Luke's hand heartily. "Hello, mate. You must be the lucky bloke who stole this beautiful lass' heart. I'm Liam."

"Luke," he said. "I'm so sorry, but for the life of me, I can't remember what Dalilah said about how you're related to her. That's all so confusing for me."

"Not a problem, mate. Her grandmother is the sister to my grandfather. I guess that makes us cousins several times removed or something of the sort. But she's a Gallagher, so that's right good enough for me. Family is family, isn't it?"

At that, he picked up my suitcases, and started to wheel another of my suitcases behind him. We walked through the airport parking lot to Liam's vehicle, which was a Mercedes SUV. Luke raised his eyebrows, although I don't know why he was surprised. I had warned him about Liam's wealth when we were on the plane on the way over here.

I knew that Luke was intimidated, and I hoped that he wouldn't be. I squeezed his hand, and both of us rode in the backseat of Liam's SUV, much to his dismay.

"Oh, come on, mates, I don't smell bad, do I? You're making me feel like a bloody chauffeur."

"I'm sorry, Liam," I said. "It's been a long, strange trip, and we're both disoriented. I hope you don't mind if we ride in the back together."

Liam shook his head. "Crikey. Oh, well, I guess if you both have that bug up your arse, I can't do much about it, can I?"

In spite of myself, I suppressed a giggle. I wasn't going to tell Luke, but I was digging Liam's accent and Britishisms.

Liam hummed a tune while we drove along through heavy traffic. "I suppose you two are pretty exhausted, aren't you?" he asked, looking in the rear-view mirror at the two of us huddled together in the back seat. The movement of the car was making me feel like I wanted to hurl. Which was really an expected thing, considering all of the stress that was going on, combined with my hormones going wild.

"Exhausted isn't the word," I said. "We're both jet-lagged, and I, for one, am feeling like I've been hit by a semi."

"Well, that's too bad," he said. "I'm looking to sign a new band, so I'm going to a club tonight. If you two feel up to it, you're welcome to come, of course. But something tells me that you both are going to be staying at home."

"You're going to a club to see about a band?" I said. Liam was the CEO of his massively successful record label, Gallagher Records, so I was surprised that he was still doing things like scouting his own talent for the label.

"Of course," he said. "I have to stay hungry, don't I? Besides, even hard-working CEOs have to have a little fun once in awhile, don't we?"

"Sure, of course," I said. "Maybe Luke and I will feel up to coming with you." Suddenly, that sounded like just the thing that I needed. It just might take my mind off of what was going on.

Luke and I had decided that we had to go ahead and live our lives the way that we were in the States, which meant that neither of us took an assumed name. After talking it through, we realized that was the only thing that we could do, as both us were going to concentrate on getting back into the art scene in London. So, there couldn't be any kind of shielding of our identities. We also decided that we had to live our normal lives. That would mean going to clubs with Liam when the situation called for it.

I actually hadn't heard from Nottingham since I left the night that he beat me. This surprised me, yet didn't surprise me at the same time. It was as if that night broke the fever that he had that made him obsessed with me in the first place. Nevertheless, I still knew, in my heart and gut, that if he found out about the baby, he would become obsessed about the child. It would be his perfect method of revenge, getting his hands on the kid.

Beyond that, Luke and I had no good answers. Usually, I could think my way out of a situation like this one, but the extreme stress and the hormones coursing through my body was making my thinking extremely foggy. At the back of my mind, I knew that there was a solution. I knew that there was. I just had to take my mind off of my stress and confusion, and I hoped that getting settled into Liam's home would give me the presence of mind to figure it out.

"What kind of band are you looking at?" Luke asked Liam.

"It's a band that has a really retro sound. I can't really explain it, except that the sound is something out of the early 1980s. I have a good sense that retro is going to be making a comeback. Everything old is new again, right?"

"Punk or New Wave?" Luke asked.

"Fusion of both, with a little bit of Ska mixed in. I have a feeling that, with the right promotion, this band has the potential to make it big."

Luke looked at me. "Dalilah, what do you think? Are you feeling up to going to the club tonight?"

"I am, Luke. It might do both of us a lot of good."

"Okay, then," he said. "Liam, we'd like to join you tonight."

Liam smiled at both of us, and nodded his head. "Right. Well, I guess you two don't have a stick up your arse after all."

Luke squeezed my hand, and we soon arrived at Liam's home, which was in the Surrey suburb. It was an enormous Tudor-style home, with a brick façade, a circular drive with an enormous three-tiered fountain in the middle of the drive, and a perfectly manicured lawn. It was the type of home that I was used to, growing up. Luke, on the other hand, was sitting next to me, looking more intimidated than ever.

# Chapter Five

## LUKE

Everything was happening so fast, I had very little time to get my bearings. But, I would have to say, that because Liam was intimidating to me for a variety of reasons, I was starting to regret my decision to come here. Thinking back, I thought that, maybe, just maybe, we should have stood our ground in New York City and let the chips fall where they may. It was a big risk, of course, but so was what we were doing. It was never in my constitution to run from things. I liked to meet problems head-on.

But Dalilah was in charge. She was the one facing the impossible situation, despite the fact that I probably was the father of the baby. So, she was the one who had to decide on our course of action.

Now, here we were, in London. I had never even traveled overseas, so I felt more than a little disoriented by it all. Even though I was used to a large city, being a New Yorker for many years, I still felt just a little bit out of sorts as we drove through the city to get to Liam's home in the London suburb of Surrey.

Liam himself was a little bit intimidating. Not his demeanor. He was friendly enough. But the fact that he was wealthy and handsome, and he didn't look at Dalilah like a cousin should. And the fact that they were only distant relatives, not close kin, made this whole situation seem

ANNIE JOCOBY

even more threatening. I trusted Dalilah, of course, but, at the same time, I knew competition when I saw it, and Liam was definitely that.

So, when Dalilah and I arrived at Liam's mansion in Surrey, I was feeling wary, along with my general feelings of being out of sorts and stressed. I wasn't exactly looking forward to going to the club that night, either. I just wanted to relax at home, and try to get settled in. But Dalilah seemed to want to go, so we were going to end up going.

THAT NIGHT, DALILAH AND I ENDED UP at a noisy London club. I was feeling much more comfortable by then, as I had a few hits of pot before coming. I had to admit, I missed getting high, and it was something that was always relaxing for me. Dalilah, of course, didn't partake in the festivities.

For Liam's part, he was all business that night at the club. More than one beautiful woman came up and tried to hit on him, but he waved them all away. We waited for the band, called The Pixxillators, to get on the stage, and they soon did appear. All of the guys in the band looked like old-fashioned eighties musicians. The lead singer was dressed in white, with a t-shirt that had holes in it, and he was extremely skinny. His hair was spiked in all directions, and he played a guitar. There was also a keyboard player with a fedora, dread locks and heavy makeup. The bassist had black hair with white tips, and black fingernails. The drummer wore a stocking cap, and was shirtless.

The sound was just as Liam had described it. They were a little bit punk, a bit New Wave, and several songs had strong reggae and Ska influences. Liam sat, silently, watching the band. Dalilah appeared to be having a good time, and, in spite of myself, I started to relax just a little bit. I couldn't help but think that this outing was going to help Dalilah and me, because it seemed to relax both of us. Us relaxing was important, because I hoped that we would be able to think just a little bit more clear about our situation if our stress-induced fog lifted.

After the band played for about 45 minutes, they took a break, and Liam turned to Dalilah and me. "So, what do you think?"

"They sound great," I said. "A fresh sound, really. If that kind of music is making a comeback, you should probably think about signing them."

Dalilah nodded her head in agreement.

"Well, I'm going to try to sign them, there's no doubt about that." He looked around the crowd, which was enjoying hearing the band. He saw somebody from across the room, and looked troubled. "Crikey. I hope he doesn't come over here."

"Who?"

"There's this arsehole who I had to sack recently for embezzling from the company." He shook his head. "He's been stalking me ever since. Every time I go to a club to check out a new band, he's usually there. And he usually tries to come up and beg for his position back."

Dalilah had a look on her face that was not discernible. She seemed like she was lost in thought.

"What is it, Dalilah?" I asked. I knew, by then, when Dalilah was having a brainstorm, and the look on her face said that her wheels were turning.

"Blackmail him," she said. "That's it! That's it, Luke! That's it!"

"What?" I had no idea what tripped her trigger, but she was clearly thinking hard about something.

"You and I have to find something on Nottingham. We have to find something, and use it to blackmail him. It has to be something good, too."

"Okay," I said. "How do you propose that we do this?"

She was tugging on my shirt sleeve. "Liam was just talking about embezzlement. White collar crime." She turned to Liam. "Why isn't that guy in prison if he was embezzling from the company?"

"The case is still pending. He lawyered up, as you Americans like to say. He has one of the best barristers in the country defending him."

"But he probably will end up in prison?" Dalilah said. "Right?"

"With any luck, he will," Liam said.

"Luke," Dalilah said to me. "Nottingham is incredibly corrupt. Do you agree with that?"

"Of course," I said.

"What are the chances that he might be involved with something that is illegal? Like, maybe, insider trading or something like that?"

"With that guy, I wouldn't be surprised about anything." I had no idea what she was thinking, though. It still seemed to be a bit of a long shot that Nottingham was involved in something illegal, and an even more long shot that Dalilah would be able to prove it.

Dalilah, though, was looking more excited. "I don't know if you know this, Luke, but I speak five languages fluently. French, Spanish, German, Italian and, of course, English. I also don't think that Nottingham knows this."

"Okay," I said. "And..."

"Well, I remember something now. When I was married to him, I overheard a conversation that he was having in German with a guy who was working at a pharmaceutical company in Bonn. He was talking really quietly, but you know that I'm a nosy bitch, so I did catch snippets of what he was saying."

I took a sip of my drink and waited for her to continue.

"There seemed to be a stock tip that he was receiving from the guy. I heard him say something about the FDA, but it was very difficult to hear everything he said, because he was almost whispering. But I did note that, within a day or so after talking with this guy, Nottingham did some trading of some of his pharmaceutical stocks. What if that guy on the other end of the line was telling Nottingham about a drug that wasn't going to be approved, and Nottingham dumped the stocks of the company? He could go to prison for that."

I shook my head. "I don't know, Dalilah. It's a long shot for sure. Plus, a guy like Nottingham could probably beat those charges, anyhow. How often do these rich guys go to prison?"

"More often than you think. If they could put Martha Stewart away, they could put anyone away. Think about that."

"Okay, then, what's the plan? How do you prove it?"

"Oh, god, it would be so easy. I could crack Nottingham's password within a couple of hours at the most. I could get into his system and look into the trading that he's done, and look for something suspicious. Some kind of heavy trading that would coincide with an FDA announcement of a certain drug, and nail him to the wall. Or, rather, use it as leverage for him to divorce me without laying any claims to the child."

I still felt skeptical. "It sounds like the best plan we got so far, but that's not saying much. I mean, you're asking the man to give up claims to his legal child. Do you really think that he's going to roll over because of an inconsequential threat?"

"Inconsequential threat? A prison sentence wouldn't be inconsequential, Luke. Especially for a guy like him. He's so into his image and what people think of him. Not to mention the fact that, if he goes to prison, he will have to also pay a large fine and his company would suffer financially. Anything that would hit him in his pocketbook would be something that he would take seriously. Money-hungry doesn't begin to describe that man."

Liam was listening intently, his hand on his chin. "Fill me in, mate. I might be able to help out with what you're thinking of doing."

Dalilah opened my mouth to start telling Liam the whole story, knowing that her dad told Liam next to nothing about my situation, but the band was coming back from its break and was starting the second set. Liam's attention was, once again, focused on the band.

# Chapter Six

## DALILAH

I was no longer paying attention to the band. I was too excited. The more I thought about it, the more I got excited about the plan. It could work, if my suspicions were true. I only wished that I would've thought about it before. Looking back, I wondered why I didn't think about the blackmail angle before that moment. But, then again, it wasn't anything that I thought twice about at the time. It just seemed to be in keeping with his overall demeanor and the way that he was. He was so corrupt and money-hungry, I just figured that he was doing something shady. I didn't know exactly what, and I was ashamed to say, I didn't really care.

I squeezed Luke's hand. He was starting to look excited, as well, almost as if he was starting to believe that my plan might work.

After the band finished its set, Liam announced that he was going to meet with them behind the scenes. "Would you like to come with me, mate?" he asked me. And then he smiled. "Who knows? Having a beautiful woman with me might increase my chances of signing these blokes."

I smiled. "I'm sure that you can sign them. After all, your company is one of the top ones in the world. They should jump at any offer you make them."

"One would think. But these blokes have a ton of international interest. I'm just one of many who are trying to get them. Everybody sees their potential."

"Okay," I said, taking Luke's hand. "Come on, Luke, let's go and meet the boys."

Liam shook his head. "Just you, lass." He turned to Luke. "Sorry, mate. Dalilah will be an asset for me with these blokes. You, not so much. No offense. It has something to do with the fact that they have penises and so do you. Dalilah, on the other hand, does not have a penis, and what she does have is stunning." He winked, and I felt uncomfortable.

"Uh, maybe I should stay here with Luke," I said. "I mean..." And then I thought about it. Liam was nice enough to let Luke and me stay with him, free of charge, while we figured out our mess. Was I really not going to do something as simple as go back with him to meet these boys?

Luke looked pissed, and I didn't blame him. "I'm sorry, Luke. I need to go back there with him. Liam's doing a lot for us by allowing us to stay with him. I hope you understand."

Luke said nothing, but just shrugged. I felt awful. It seemed that Luke was feeling threatened by Liam as it was, and this certainly wasn't helping matters much at all. To say the very least.

I looked back as I made my way backstage. Luke was sitting in his seat, chomping some ice in his drink. To my dismay, I saw a gorgeous woman join him at his table. To my further dismay, he didn't seem to dissuade her from joining him for a drink.

I sighed. I felt that I was walking a tightrope, between trying to keep Luke happy and trying to show my appreciation for Liam. And, when Liam put his arm around me, as we made our way through the crowd, I felt even more uncomfortable.

Finally, we got to the backstage, and, sure enough, when I walked back there with Liam, all four of the musicians looked at me appreciatively. I felt like the lead singer was undressing me with his eyes.

Liam shook the boy's hand. "Hello there, mate, my name is Liam Gallagher. I'm CEO of Gallagher Records." He handed the kid his card. "And this is Dalilah. She's a distant cousin of mine, and a big fan of yours."

Inwardly, I cringed. I had never even heard of this band until that evening, so I didn't know any of their songs. Granted, I liked what I heard, but I knew nothing about them. I was afraid that this kid would start asking me about which song I liked the best or what I liked about their music. I didn't have an answer for that, aside from the songs that I heard in their set.

The boy raised his eyebrows at me. "Hello, Dalilah. My name is Neil." He looked nervous, and blushed furiously. I was amused, as he seemed just a little bit shy. Very much unlike his onstage demeanor, I thought, wryly.

The other boys came up and introduced themselves as Derrick, Nate, and Simon. All of them made me feel welcome. A little too welcome, really.

"Okay," Liam said, after the introductions were done. "What do you mates say we meet somewhere and talk about the possibility that you might sign with my record label?"

"Maybe," Derrick said. "If you bring Dalilah along with you."

I was feeling even more uncomfortable. I wasn't prepared to be used as bait for these young musicians, and I, quite frankly, didn't like it.

"Of course," Liam said. "That goes without saying, mate."

I started to open my mouth, but Liam just put his hand on my shoulder and squeezed. I suddenly wondered if my staying with Liam had some kind of strings attached. Strings that I was heretofore unaware of. Strings that Luke would be very upset about, to say the very least.

Liam whispered. "Just come to dinner with us, gorgeous. That's all you have to do."

"Okay," I said. "But it ends there. I'm not going to do anything else. Got that?" I was annoyed, and I immediately started thinking that Luke and I would maybe have to get a flat of our own if Liam asked me to do something other than have dinner with these guys.

"Of course," he said. "I'm not a pimp." Then he smiled, and I was wondering about that. Something told me that Liam got his way a lot with his looks and charm, and he obviously thought that I would fall into line as well. I would have to disabuse of that notion as soon as possible.

"You better not be," I said.

32

"Well," Liam said to the boys. "Why don't we meet for dinner tomorrow night? Glasshouse on Parade is an excellent restaurant. We could meet at 7 PM, and talk about you blokes signing with my label."

Neil nodded, but he wasn't looking at Liam. He was boring his eyes into me. Undressing me with his eyes. I squirmed and felt myself blushing bright red. I looked around, half thinking that Luke might be around the corner, and would see the way this kid was looking at me, and not be happy at all. At all.

Derrick stepped in. "We'll be there tomorrow night." He put his arm around Neil. "Come on, Neil. Let's go and meet some of the fans who have backstage passes." He turned to me, and shook my hand. "Dalilah, it was a pleasure." He shook Liam's hand next. "Mr. Gallagher, thank you very much for your offer. We'll see you tomorrow night."

And, at that, the boys disappeared into the crowd of people who were starting to gather. They starting signing autographs and posing for pictures.

I gathered my breath and glared at Liam. "Liam, I'll have you know that you've put me into a real pickle. You saw the way that Neil looked at me. Now, you want to bring me along to this dinner. I feel like a piece of rare steak being used to lure a lion into a trap."

"There's no trap here, young Dalilah," Liam said. "I'm just trying to get these boys signed onto my label. They're going to hit it big, and I want to be a part of that."

"You're avoiding what I'm saying," I said. "Either that, or your deliberately trying to make my words to be something that they're not. At any rate, I think that you have less than honorable reasons for my being at this dinner tomorrow night. Luke will not be pleased."

"I'm not concerned about that," he said. "I'm sorry, Dalilah, but I want to get this boys signed. And if you help me do that, then that's all the better." Then he smiled. "I hope that you really don't mind doing this one thing for me. Family needs to stick together and help each other out, right?"

The implication to me was clear. He was helping me, now it was my turn to help him. I had started staying with him for not even one day, and I already was being asked to repay his favor.

I sighed. Nothing ever came free, of course. Not that I thought that it did. But, I did wish that I didn't feel so uncomfortable doing this. My gut was telling me that it just wasn't right.

But I ignored my gut and told him "okay. I'll go with you tomorrow night. I'm assuming that I have to tell Luke to stay home. Am I correct about that?"

"Goes without saying, lass."

I shook my head. This whole thing was starting to remind me of Nottingham. I thought about the night of Luke's premiere, when I was being held out as some type of rote doll for him to impress his friends. Now, here I was, being asked to do something similar.

"Well, then, let's get out of here. Luke's out there, all by himself, waiting for me to come back."

We made our way back to the table. To my dismay, the gorgeous woman who had walked over to Luke when Liam and I were walking back stage was still there at the table, hanging onto every word Luke was saying.

I looked at Luke, and he looked back at me. He frowned and narrowed his eyes. I read his expression perfectly. Luke was no dummy. He knew what Liam was trying to do. And, as I figured, he wasn't much happy about it.

"Marcella," he said to the woman. "It was very nice to meet you. My girlfriend is back here at the table," he said, motioning to me.

I put my hand out, and she shook it. She smiled. "Very nice to meet you. Luke here is a fascinating guy." She looked back at Luke. "Don't forget to call me on Monday."

"I won't," he said.

I gave Luke a look like *what the hell is going on here?*

Luke just raised his eyebrows at me and said nothing.

I sat down and put my arm around him. "Honey," I said. "You're going to be mad, I know. But I'm going out to dinner with Liam tomorrow night with those boys from The Pixxillators."

Luke just shrugged. "Have fun." He looked annoyed.

I didn't say anything. I was waiting for him to explain the mysterious Marcella, but he just took a sip of his beer and started chatting up Liam. They started talking about futbol, a topic that I had little interest in, but that Luke apparently knew a lot about. After about a half hour of that, I started to feel bored and more than a little bit annoyed.

The night dragged on. I started to feel more than a little bit warm, and almost claustrophobic. The club was jammed with people, and more were streaming through the door all through the night. I never had much fun in loud sweaty clubs, so I found myself wanting to just go home.

Finally, at around 3 AM, Liam called his driver, and we all headed for the exit and into a waiting limo.

When we finally arrived at his home, Luke and I went to our designated room. I lay down on the bed, exhausted and spent. I was tired all the time, anyhow, due to my pregnancy. But, add in jet-lag and one very long night at a very noisy and crowded club, and you have the recipe for physical exhaustion. I knew that I would be sleeping well.

As soon as my head hit the pillow, I was out.


THE NEXT DAY, I WOKE UP AROUND NOON. Luke was already up, and was sitting on the terrace, which was right outside the bedroom, his legs up on the ledge. He had a sketch pad on his lap, and was working away on sketching the landscape that was in front of him. Every so once in awhile, he put his hand on his chin and had a faraway look on his face.

I went out onto the terrace with him, and sat down. He smiled, and put his arm around me. "Good morning, Dalilah. How did you sleep?"

"Very well. Liam's mattress is so comfortable."

Luke nodded. He still had his right arm around me, while his left hand was still furiously working on his sketch. "This place is so beautiful and peaceful. It really inspires me." He took a deep breath. "I wish that I had a place like this to go to in New York. I thought that I would miss the city, but I really don't."

I knew what he was talking about. Liam's house was set on about 10 acres of land, and the terrace was facing a forest that was covered in snow that shimmered in the sunlight.

I drew a breath. "Marcella is certainly pretty."

Luke nodded his head, and barely acknowledged my statement. He still looked lost in thought, as he continued to sketch the gorgeous grass, trees and nature that were within view.

I grabbed Luke's knee and squeezed hard. "Who is she?"

Luke sighed. "Dalilah, I think that you're jealous. Join the club. Liam might be your cousin, but I don't like the way that he looks at you. I don't trust him. I don't know what he has in mind in inviting you to dinner, and only you, but I don't think that he has honorable intentions."

I knew that he was right. "I know. I guess that you and I should just start looking for a place of our own in London proper. Liam seems to be expecting something in return for giving us a place to stay. Not that I'm going to be giving it. Not at all. But it seems like he might be expecting it."

"Dalilah, I trust you. Implicitly. So, it offends me that you don't seem to trust me just as much." Then he sighed. "Marcella is somebody that I met back in New York. At my show. I thought she looked familiar, and so, when she came up to me, I had to place her face. She reminded me that she was part of a group that I was talking to at my show."

I felt excited as he talked. "Oh, that's great. Does she know people here in town who might be able to help you?"

"She does. At any rate, she wants me to call her."

Then he looked away, squinting into the sunlight.

I felt uncomfortable. There was clearly something on his mind.

"Are you going to call her?" I asked.

"Of course," he said. "That's why I'm here, isn't it? To try to get connections to get me re-established. I'm really trying to salvage anything from the exposure I've gotten from my show. Otherwise, this entire mess that we're in would be for naught. That bothers me."

I knew what he was saying. All that I did, I did so that he would get his chance in the spotlight. This entire mess – my pregnancy, the possibility that Nottingham would have claims to the baby, my beating, Luke's criminal charge – could have been avoided if I just would have called Nottingham's bluff. Luke wouldn't have had his chance, though. So, it was important that something positive could be salvaged from my actions.

"So, what's on your mind?" I asked him.

36

ANNIE JOCOBY

"You, Dalilah. You're on my mind. Don't get me wrong, I'm really glad that you had a brainstorm about blackmailing that bastard into giving you what you want. But I really wish that there was something a bit more ironclad that we could use. Something that doesn't have the possibility of backfiring on you."

I got quiet. "I know. I realize that my hands aren't clean. Or, at least, my hands won't be clean if I do this. But do you have a better idea right now? Aside from us running for the rest of our lives?"

He put his hands behind his head. "No. No, I don't. So, let's try it. But you're playing chess with the master, here. He always seems to be just one step ahead. That seems to be the pattern. He's probably going to be one step ahead here as well. I, for one, am tired of always playing defense with this guy. I'm tired of us having to constantly figure out a way out of a trap that he has set. For once, I would like to put him on the run."

"Me too. That's why my plan is so beautiful. If it works, then he will be the one on the run, not us."

"And if it doesn't work?"

"I guess that we'll have more to worry about than ever."

Luke sighed. "I guess I have to put my trust in you and trust that you know what you're doing here. But it just seems that, no matter what happens, we're doing something underhanded. If I'm not using a fake badge to try to find out personal information about Nottingham, then you're trying to do something clearly illegal – hacking – to possibly get information that might be damning. And you're just speculating that Nottingham has done something wrong. He might be as clean as a whistle. But you're going to break the law to find out. What's wrong with this picture?"

I raised my eyebrow, halfway tempted to tell him that Nick literally killed a man, or made him commit suicide at any rate, to get Scotty out of a jam. *That* was underhanded and illegal. What I was planning to do was child's play in comparison.

But I didn't say anything about that. Bringing that up would just put fuel on the fire, which I really didn't want to do.

"Again," I said. "Do you have a better idea?"

Luke just frowned and shook his head. "No. Other than doing

things above-board – hiring a lawyer and letting the chips fall where they may – I got nothing. So, let's try it."

I put my hand on his leg. He felt so far away at that moment, even though he was sitting right next to me. He absent-mindedly took my hand, and rubbed it while he sketched some more.

Finally, Liam knocked on the bedroom door. "Dalilah, Luke. Are you alive in there?"

I went to the door and opened it. "Hi, Liam. What's up?"

"Well, I had my chef make some Eggs Benedict for the two of you. Not to mention French Toast and freshly squeezed orange juice. Needless to say, all of that was fed to the dogs." Liam had two German Short-haired Pointers that he had rescued from a nearby shelter. "At any rate, it's now lunch time. What would you like? My chef can make anything at all."

"I'm not really hungry," I said, rubbing my stomach.

"Be that as it may, you need to eat. Especially in your condition. And what about Luke? What would he like?"

"Surprise me," he said.

Liam just sighed. "Why do I have the feeling that the two of you are going to be a pain in my arse?" He shook his head, and headed down the stairs. "Meet me on the main terrace in a half hour. We'll have lunch and I can catch up on exactly what is going on with you guys, and why, exactly, you're here. I might be able to help."

I had a feeling that Liam was right about that. He probably would be able to help us. He was a Gallagher, and, as such, he probably had above-average intelligence and above-average duplicity.

Luke, however, just rolled his eyes. I was getting the feeling that Luke really just wanted to go back home and face this entire situation above-board. He didn't know Nottingham like I knew Nottingham, and Luke really didn't know, in general, how men like Nottingham rolled. I did. I knew far too many people like Nottingham in my life – money-hungry, duplicitous, greedy, cruel – and I knew how little chance I would have against him if I didn't have something in my arsenal to use when push came to shove. As it inevitably would.

. . .

38

In a half hour, Luke and I made our way downstairs to Liam's magnificent main terrace. It was a beautiful day, surprisingly warm for it being February, and the surroundings were very peaceful. I took a deep breath, inhaling the fresh air. I had almost forgotten what fresh air smelled like and what quiet sounded like. In that moment, I almost forgot my misgivings about Liam, and inwardly felt grateful that I was able to get away to such a place.

Liam's personal chef had prepared fried chicken for us, along with new potatoes with cheese, and a green salad. I eagerly dug into my food. I hadn't realized until just that moment that I was famished. Luke did the same, and Liam looked at both of us, clearly amused.

"I knew you would be hungry," he said, pouring a Mimosa for Luke and himself. I satisfied myself with some freshly squeezed orange juice. "Now, tell me exactly what's going on. Your dad just told me that the two of you had run into a bit of a predicament in the States, but didn't exactly say what."

"Ugh," I said. I didn't much feel like talking about any of it. It was all just too stressful for me to even think about. "Well, let's start from the very beginning. There's this man named Nottingham...." I then launched into the whole sorry tale, from the time I met Nottingham until the present day. The entire story took me about an hour to tell, and Liam, for his part, listened quietly and really tried to absorb all of what was going on.

"Well, lass," Liam finally said, after I finished the story. "Sounds like you got into a right jam with that bastard. What's your next move?"

"Well," I said, "I need to start some hacking into his computer. I don't know the password, of course, and he changes it all the time. Like every day. But that's not a problem for me. I know that I can get in past his security safeguards and try to figure if there is anything on there which would incriminate him and take a screen shot of it. I'm not even sure if there is anything on there, but that's what I need to do."

"Ah, blackmail," Liam said. "One of the oldest and most tried and true way of getting what you want." He seemed to tacitly approve of what I was about to do. "Well, good luck with all of that. Let me know if there's anything at all that I can do to help you out."

"I will," I said.

At that, Liam went to work out in his gym.

Luke took my hand, and rubbed it thoughtfully. Then he sighed. "I really hope that this works, Dalilah. But what happens if he's the one blackmailing you? What if you threaten to turn him in, and he decides that he's going to go full-throttle on the custody issue if you don't back off? Who's going to blink first?"

"I've thought about that," I said. "And I think that he will. His legal position with this child is far from settled. I think that he will know that, just from talking with his attorney. On the other hand, if I find on his computer what I'm hoping to find, then I will have a much more solid hand against him then he would with me. Therefore, I think that I will have the upper hand with him, if push comes to shove."

"And what if Nottingham decides to do something even more drastic or devious? What then?"

"What do you think that he'll do?"

"Oh, geez, that guy is capable of just about anything. Who knows? Maybe he'll threaten your dad somehow."

I drew a breath. I doubted that Nottingham had a way of threatening my father, but he might have a way of threatening Nick. Perhaps Nottingham also had a way of finding out what Nick did all those years ago. It took me a long time to find that video, because it was pretty well scrubbed from Nick's computer. But I did find it. What if Nottingham had his own capabilities in that department?

"Well, I guess that's just a risk that I have to take," I said, but I started to feel uneasy again about my plan. The very last thing that I wanted to do was get Nick in trouble.

But, then again, it was a long shot that Nottingham could ever find out about that. He would have to be looking, and know what he was looking for and why. I really thought that I would be safe.

I hoped and prayed that I would be, anyhow.

# Chapter Seven

That night, I got dolled up and went with Liam to the restaurant to meet the boys from the Pixxallators. They were already there, waiting for us, having already gotten ales and beers. Neil, for his part, came right up to me and put his arm around me. "Dalilah," he said. "You can't imagine how glad I am to see you tonight."

I smiled, and put my hand out. "You too, Neil. Uh, let's sit down."

Liam ordered for everybody around the table, and sipped his scotch and got right down to business. "Okay, guys. I want you to sign with my label. I know that you have other prospects, so let's talk terms here."

Neil just kinda snickered, and put his hand on my shoulder. "Well, yes, yes we do have other offers. A lot of other offers. All the other labels have just talked about how they're going to promote us, what kind of advance money they're going to give us, how much creative control and all of that. I'm sure you're going to do the same." Then he raised an eyebrow and leered at me. "But you have something they don't. And that's a beautiful woman to sweeten the pot."

I drew a breath. Neil had not yet done anything that would be considered inappropriate, as far as touching me. But he was staring hungrily at my breasts, and I could tell that he was just moments away from grabbing at them.

I shot a look at Liam, and he looked non-plussed by Neil's obvious overtures. Finally, he just said "Dalilah isn't included in the package, of course. I'm not a pimp. But I can give you favorable terms. I've done a bit of research, and I know that you're being pursued by EMI, Sony, Universal and Warner Music Group. You're also being pursued by quite a few independent labels as well. I know that they're offering you, and I know that you're close to signing with EMI. I'm prepared to offer you everything that EMI is offering you, plus a great deal more creative control." Liam then launched into the terms that he was willing to give the boys, and Derrick, Nate and Simon looked impressed. Neil, however, didn't.

"No go, mate," Neil finally said. "You'll have to do better than that. You have to throw Dalilah in, just for one night. One night with her, and I'm ready to sign with you. Otherwise, I'm going with EMI. And I'm the leader of this band, and what I say goes."

"Well, that's too bad," I said to Neil. "I'm not a part of the deal, and I never will be. I really don't even know why I came to this dinner, to be honest. I certainly didn't come here to be treated like a piece of sirloin steak."

"Well then, the deal is off," Neil said. "Not that we even had a deal at all, but I'm ending the negotiations right this very minute."

Liam sighed. "You want to play hardball, mate? I'm giving you much more favorable terms than any of the other labels, not to mention complete creative control. I'm taking a risk in doing that too, because, quite frankly, I think that you blokes need some kind of guidance in that department if you want to make it huge. You're going to throw that all away because you can't have a night with a pregnant lady?" Liam just shook his head. "You go right ahead, then. But you're going to regret it."

"Wait," Neil said, turning to me. "You're pregnant?"

"I am," I said. "I'm a few months along."

Neil looked like somebody had just bit him hard. "Oh, I'm sorry," he said, suddenly looking like the silly boy that he was. "I meant no disrespect." Then he turned to Liam, and, to my utmost relief, he said "Sorry, mate, for saying all that. The negotiations are back on."

"I thought so," Liam said. "Now, let's get on the same page."

At that, Liam and the boys started talking about all the terms that each of them were willing to accept. I held my breath, hoping that Neil wasn't going to change his mind about having me as a stipulation to signing. I was also grateful that, when push came to shove, Liam went to bat for me. I was really afraid that Liam would try to push me into a situation that I just couldn't accept, and then punish me for not accepting.

By the end of the evening, the boys had ended up signing a contract with Gallagher records. "You won't regret this," he said to the group. "You're going to be huge."

Neil smiled, and looked at me. "Oh, lass, you're missing out. You could have told all your friends that you had wild monkey sex with me before I became famous. Alas, it's not to be."

I nodded my head, thinking, secretly, that I wasn't missing out on much. I had the world's greatest lover, Luke, and that was really all that I was thinking about.


ON THE WAY BACK TO LIAM'S PLACE, we had a long drive ahead of us, because the restaurant was about forty-five minutes away from Liam's Surrey home. Liam hummed softly and then said "sorry about all that mess, Dalilah. About Neil, I mean. He was a little blunt. I wasn't expecting that, to be honest. Of course, then again, drunk people are prone to say what's on their mind, aren't they?"

"You might say that."

"Well, you handled yourself really well. Luke would be proud. At any rate, thanks for coming along with me."

"I'm not sure what good I did, but you're welcome."

"So," Liam said. "What can I do to help you out some? I know that there must be something that I can do."

"You're doing a ton just letting us stay with you and allowing us to decompress. I really couldn't ask for more. But I will tell you that Luke is a musician and a song-writer, although his art takes precedent in his life. Maybe he could play some of his songs for you?"

"Of course," he said. "I'll listen to them. But no promises. If they aren't any good, then I'm not going to do anything with them. But if they're good, then I might be able to sell them to some of the groups that are already signed to my label."

"That's all I can ask," I said.

We finally pulled into the driveway. The light was on in my room. I was looking forward to just being with Luke, and finally getting a chance to relax just a little bit. Being with the boys that night made me realize how much I craved being with Luke. There wasn't any way that I would jeopardize what I had with him, which was the main reason why what Neil was proposing was way off-limits. I would have left Liam's house if he tried to push the issue with me.

Of that, I was sure.

# Chapter Eight

## LUKE

Dalilah had just left to be with Liam and meet the band out at a fancy restaurant, and I was feeling out of sorts about it. I trusted her not to hurt me again, although I wasn't entirely sure why I trusted her. After all, she did all these things behind my back with Nottingham. Who was to say that she was really above doing something just as devious, if it meant making Liam happy?

Then I realized that, with my thinking along those lines, I needed some kind of way to come to terms with all that had happened. I was surprised that I was feeling this way –having a nagging feeling that Dalilah wasn't to be trusted. She would be more than upset if she ever was clued in to how I was feeling, though, so I didn't bring it up to her.

I also realized that I might have been feeling that Dalilah was up to no good because of all the devious things that she had done. Things that I didn't even know about until well after the fact. I had no clue that she and Nottingham had a relationship, at all, until all the shit had hit the fan. Then, come to find out that Dalilah was playing Nottingham behind my back all along. That rankled, even though she did it for me. But it did seem that she was just a bit too much of a mercenary for me. It upset me that she apparently wasn't above playing people to get what she wanted.

Would she play me as well? Or, perhaps worse, would she play somebody else if it meant that the ends of doing so would be favorable to her or me? It seemed that Dalilah did truly love me, and I knew that I truly loved her. But, with a woman who had no compunction in manipulating others for her own gain, was it only a matter of time until I became a casualty of her games?

Then again, was I any better? Marcella had made it clear that she wanted in my pants, yet I was going to see her anyhow. I didn't tell Dalilah that Marcella had propositioned me. Which she did, in no uncertain terms. But Marcella had the kind of connections that I was looking for, as she was a member of a group of eclectic artists who were making a splash in the London art scene. I wanted to become a part of that group, and get Dalilah involved as well. It seemed to me that I would be able to network in that group, and find my footing and be on my way to finding my audience once more.

I felt like such a hypocrite. I didn't entirely trust Dalilah, because she had proven that she could manipulate with the best of them. But I wasn't above my own manipulation.

I wished that there was some way for Dalilah and me to not only get out of our mess, and her trap, but to also find our footing in the art world, all without compromising any of our core values. But, it seemed that, with every passing day, it was more and more unlikely that we were going to find our way out without one, or both, of us doing something that we probably shouldn't.

Then it struck me exactly what bothered me the most about the whole situation. What bothered me was that I thought about the issues. I obsessed about getting my hands dirty, and about the ethics of everything that we were doing. Dalilah seemed to be undisturbed by it all. As if she completely justified all of the dirty business in her head.

For all I knew, that was exactly what was going on. Dalilah *was* justifying all of the trickery and deception, and honestly didn't see anything wrong with any of it.

It was then that I realized that maybe, just maybe, Dalilah wasn't the one for me after all.

. . .

By the time Dalilah finally arrived home, I was itching for a fight. It finally felt like it was time to clear the air with her, and I was going to, at long last, tell her all that was on my mind.

She came in the door around 2 AM, looking tired and blue. For a second, I lost my nerve. She was so beautiful, and she looked so lost and vulnerable.

But I had to say my piece.

"Dalilah," I began. "I need to talk to you."

"Luke, before you say anything, I need you to know that nothing happened with me and those boys. One of the boys clearly wanted something to happen, but I put a stop to it really quick."

"I'm glad to hear that. But I've been sitting here and stewing, and I realized that I didn't trust you after all not to do something stupid. I hate that I don't trust you. I hate that more than anything. But, really, can you blame me?"

"What do you mean by that? Did you actually think that something was going to happen between me and Neil or any of the other boys?"

"I wasn't certain. That's what bothers me. Of course, I 99% trust you to not do anything that would damage our relationship. But there's this nagging 1% of me that believes that you would. That you would do it if it benefited you in some way. I don't want that. I want to be 100% sure that you wouldn't do something behind my back. But I never dreamed that you would do all that you did with Nottingham behind my back. Yes, it was all to benefit me, and I'm still grateful for that. But it was still devious and shady."

Dalilah had tears in her eyes. "I can't believe that I'm hearing this from you, Luke. I just can't believe it. There was never an inkling that I would do what Neil wanted me to do. Never a millisecond did I think about it, no matter if Liam wanted me to or not."

"And did Liam want you to?"

"No. He stuck up for me."

"Well, good for him," I said sarcastically. "I can't say that I'm not surprised, though. He seems the sort who would sell you out to the highest bidder."

"Why don't you like him?"

I shrugged my shoulders. "I don't know. I just don't trust him, that's all. He's a little too charming. He wants everyone to see him in a certain way, but I have a feeling that's all an act. I mean, what do you really know about him?"

"I know that he's family. And Grandma Maggie has nothing but good things to say about him. Other than that, I admit, I don't know a whole lot."

I ran my hand through my hair. "Okay, here is the problem, I think. I want to clear the air. But I admit that I'm feeling resentment towards you. I am. I feel that you got yourself into this awful quandary, and bringing my baby into it, too. All of this is through your own actions, Dalilah. Yet I'm paying the price, as is my unborn child. *Our* unborn child. I guess that I really want to hear from you that you are hesitant about all that you're doing. That you know that it's the wrong thing, but you're still going to do it because it's the only way. There must be something in your conscience that is telling you that digging a deeper hole might not turn out the way that you want it to."

Dalilah got quiet. Too quiet. Then she shook her head. "I wish that I could tell you that, Luke, but I can't lie. I do feel that the ends justify the means here. At least with Nottingham. I also think that when you're fighting against a guy like him, you have to be just as shady as he is. Just as ruthless. You can't bring a knife to a gun fight, which is what I'll be doing if I don't get down to his level. I'm sorry you can't see that."

My heart sunk at her words. To know that nothing was eating at her conscience was knowledge that I didn't really want. I wanted to see her as my Dalilah. My perfect, pristine, beautiful Dalilah. Not as some kind of modern-day Lady MacBeth, justifying her less-than-legal actions in her head. What was the term that Serena had for things that Dalilah was doing? Extralegal. A euphemism for shady and underground.

I shook my head. "I wish that I agreed with you. I really do. But I wasn't brought up that way. My sister is a different story, of course. Now I see why the two of you get along so well. You both are as intelligent as you are cunning."

I could see in Dalilah's face that my words were cutting her to the bone. "What will you have me do, Luke? What? Give this baby to Nottingham? Let him raise the child to become a mini-Blake? You want to see ruthless and cunning? You'll see it, Luke. You'll see it in our child if Nottingham gets a chance to raise this child, even part-time. If that happens, this child will leave me in the dust as far as being duplicitous and shady. Fine, Luke. You win. We go back and get a lawyer and hope to god that things turn out the way that you want. Because if they don't, you're going to know exactly what underhanded and ruthless looks like."

I put my hand in my hair. "Would that be so wrong? Maybe you should lie in the bed that you made." As soon as I said this, though, I regretted it. Dalilah's face was stricken, and she sat down on the bed. She shook her head violently, and grabbed her stomach.

"I can't believe you would say this to me," she said, as I sat down next to her and put my arm around her.

"Dalilah, I'm sorry. I'm so sorry. I didn't mean that."

"Yes you did. You did mean that. It came out of your mouth, therefore you meant it. And you can't take it back, either. You're an ungrateful bastard after all."

I took a deep breath. Maybe I *was* an ungrateful bastard. Dalilah might have made her bed with Nottingham, but, after all, she did it all for me. Perhaps I needed to give her more of a break when it came to all of that.

"No, Dalilah, I'm not ungrateful. I'm not. I'm just frustrated. It seems that you and I are continually trying to cover up and fix things by doing something that isn't legal or even right. Now you want to hack into his computer. I just wish that there was a better way of getting what we want here. That's all."

But Dalilah wasn't hearing me. Her breathing was shallow, and she continued to hold her stomach. "Luke, something isn't right," she said. "Something isn't right."

# Chapter Nine

I looked at Dalilah's pale face, and I immediately felt scared. I shook my head. "What's wrong? Tell me what's wrong?"

"I don't know. I mean, I'm having some cramping, which is normal. But I feel a little bit of wetness in my panties." She shook her head. "I'm scared, Luke. Come with me into the bathroom."

I went with her into the bathroom, and she pulled down her pants. There was a small amount of blood in her underwear.

"Okay, Dalilah," I said, as calmly as I could. "Let's go downstairs and get Liam's driver to take us to the ER. It could be nothing." In the back of my mind, though, I wondered. What if Dalilah was about to have a miscarriage? Would that be the answer to our prayers? And I immediately felt shitty for even thinking that. Selfish. Like I was praying for a life to end, just so that we could get out of our predicament.

Sure, it would make life infinitely easier. We'd just hop a plane, Dalilah would file for divorce, easy peasy. Then, if Dalilah and I could work out our current issues regarding trust and her proclivity for doing things under the table, so to speak, she and I would be married before the year was out. Neither of us would ever look back.

But, then again, emotionally, it would never be that easy. We both would be losing a child. Granted, the child was in a very early stage, and

I assumed that there would be plenty more chances for more in the future. But that really didn't make it any easier.

All those thoughts were coursing through my mind as Dalilah and I made our way down the stairs. I went to Liam's door and knocked gently. He opened it, bleary eyed.

"Hey, mate," he said. "What can I do for you at this late hour?"

"Dalilah is bleeding," I said.

At that, his eyes got huge. "I'll get dressed. Wait for me in the foyer. I won't be a second."

I went over to Dalilah, who was sitting on the floor. "How are you feeling?" I asked her.

"Okay," she said. "Aside from the bleeding, I feel fine. Minor cramping, nothing huge." She took a deep breath. "What do you think, Luke?"

I knew exactly what she was asking, and I didn't really have an answer for her. "I don't know. Let's not get ahead of ourselves until we see a doctor. As I said, it could be a minor thing. I'm not an expert, but sometimes you do bleed when you're pregnant." Even as I said that, though, I knew that I was talking out my ass. I was a 21-year-old guy who had never been a father. What the hell did I know about all of that?

Dalilah just shook her head. "Bleeding is sometimes normal, sure. I've read up on it, of course. But it could also be a sign of...." She took a deep breath. "Like you said, though, there's no cause for alarm until a doctor says something. No reason to get ahead of ourselves and assume the worst."

Both of us were silent. Neither of us dared speak about what was clearly on both our minds.

Finally, Dalilah did voice it. "Is this a blessing, Luke? I mean, if, you know, the worst happens." She shook her head. "Ok, ok, ok. Not going to think about that until a doctor checks me out."

Liam was out within a few minutes, dressed and ready. "No sense waiting for a driver. The hospital is about ten minutes away. Come on, mates. Let's go."

We piled into Liam's Mercedes and Dalilah and I sat in the back again, my arm around her, her head on my shoulder. Liam didn't protest this time about the two of us sitting in the back.

Neither of us said one word on the way to the hospital.

But I rubbed her shoulder and kissed her forehead. The earlier fight and tension was completely forgotten. I only wanted what was best for her, and for us.

I just wish that I knew exactly what that was.

# *Chapter Ten*

## DALILAH

I had no words as Luke and I were driven to the hospital. I couldn't even begin to think. Here it was, the answer to my prayers, it seemed. Maybe. But if the bleeding was a sign of a miscarriage, wouldn't that really be what was the absolute best? Wouldn't it?

I didn't know. I couldn't think. I tried, hard, not to let my mind wander to that idea until a doctor saw me and told me, definitively, what the bleeding meant. Maybe he would just say that I was okay, it was just normal spotting, not to worry.

But perhaps that wasn't the case at all. I felt ashamed and guilty, like I had willed this to happen. In the back of my mind, I secretly wished for this. It was always in the recesses of my brain, though, never in the light. I would have felt like a really horrible person if I would have wished for it.

But, come on. I was actually thinking of terminating when I first learned about it. About her. I couldn't think of the baby as an "it," I had to assign the baby a gender, and I decided just to refer to my unborn child as "her." But I was seriously considering terminating her when I first found out. I was ready to go to a clinic that day. Luke and I had fought about it, and that was the only reason why I changed my mind and chose this drastic course of action.

That was the only reason why.

Or was it?

I didn't know. I had to admit, that I was feeling more maternal and attached by the day.

But I couldn't deny that having a miscarriage would be the ultimate answer to our dilemma. I knew that Luke was thinking the same thing. That was why he was so quiet. He was thinking along the same lines. Probably wrestling with the same question.

We got to the hospital, and I was immediately taken to a room and waited for the doctor. Luke was standing next to me, as I sat on the metal table, dressing gown on, waiting for the doctor. He squeezed my hand, still not saying anything.

A nurse came in and took a urine and blood sample, and informed me that the doctor would be in shortly. I nodded my head.

About fifteen minutes later, the doctor did appear. He was an American guy, judging by his accent. His age appeared to be around 50 or so, but he was in decent shape and had a full head of salt and pepper hair. He looked at me.

"Well," he said. "You're not having a miscarriage yet. But your progesterone level does look dangerously low. We need to give you some injections so that your pregnancy can continue in a healthy way. I would also prescribe bed rest until you are out of the woods."

I took a deep breath, and looked at Luke, and then back at the doctor. "What if I don't take those injections?" I felt strangely relieved, yet conflicted all the same.

"With your progesterone level being so low, you would be at serious risk for a miscarriage."

Oh, god. Just what I didn't want to hear. I had to make a decision, here. An active decision. If I refused the injections, I was probably going to lose the baby. It wouldn't be an abortion. It wouldn't even necessarily be my fault. It would just be nature taking its course. Just as if I was a pioneer woman, and this type of thing happened. Spontaneous miscarriage. Something that Mother Nature caused for millennia, until we had modern medicine to do something about it.

It wouldn't be morally wrong. It wouldn't be murder or active killing. I wouldn't have it on my conscience.

Would I?

"How long?" I asked. "How long until I have to make this decision?"

The doctor looked perplexed. "Oh, I'm so sorry. I just assumed..." Then he shook his head. "Well, it does look like you have a day or so until your progesterone levels drop to where you are in serious danger of miscarrying. But if you want to keep your pregnancy active, then you probably should decide as soon as possible."

As soon as possible. I had to make an impossible decision as soon as possible.

I started breathing heavily. What was I going to do? What was the right decision here? All along, I thought that this would be the best outcome for everyone involved – Luke, me and the unborn child. It certainly would be the least complicated thing.

Now, here it was. Decision time. And I felt like it was the most impossible one to make.

The doctor took my hand, and said "well, at any rate, I think that I will have you admitted to the hospital for observation."

At that, he left. I knew that it would be a matter of time before the nurse came and got me and wheeled me to my room.

I gripped Luke's hand, hard.

He didn't say anything, but I saw tears in his eyes.

"What should I do, Luke?" I asked in a small voice. "I'm so scared of making the wrong decision. I'm so scared, Luke. What's the right decision here? What is it?"

Luke shook his head. "I know that you don't want to hear this from me, and I apologize in advance. But I really don't know. I wish we had a crystal ball that would tell us how this would all shake out in the future. I know what I want in my heart, and that's clearly that you should take those injections and follow the doctor's orders for bed rest. My head says something different, though."

"Me too. My heart wants to keep her. I feel that she's a part of me. But my head says something different, just like yours."

Luke smiled. "Her, huh? Funny, I was thinking the exact same thing."

I smiled back and drew a breath. "Yeah, her. I was thinking Gabriela. I always loved that name."

Luke had a faraway look on his face. The look was interminably sad. Finally, he just said "I was thinking about calling her Olivia."

I nodded, understanding. I felt tears coming to my eyes. "Olivia would be a beautiful name. It would really honor your mother."

Luke squeezed my hand again. "Come on, we can't just approach this emotionally. We have to use logic, too. I mean, there will be other chances, of course. We're both so young. And, of course, this might be the best outcome." He hung his head. "God, that sounds so bad. Like this child doesn't deserve to live because she's an inconvenience. But we have to think of it rationally, too."

I squeezed his hand back, but didn't say anything. I had no words to say, really. I couldn't verbalize what I wanted, what I thought was best, because I had no idea what that was.

Zero idea.

Finally, the nurse came in and put me in a wheelchair, and I headed to my room. Luke went to tell Liam what was going on, and, after I got to my room, Luke came up. "I sent Liam home. He's really concerned. Maybe I misjudged him a little bit."

"I know, Luke. You probably did misjudge him. But that's okay. He doesn't look at me like a relative should. And I know that we're only distantly related, so I know that you feel threatened by him a little."

"Not as much him as that Neil guy. I don't know. I didn't meet him, but I didn't like what you said about him. Anyhow, that's neither here nor there. You need to rest comfortably, and I'm going to stay here with you."

I put my head on his shoulder, and, before long, I was asleep.


"Mom?" I heard a voice say.

"What is it, Olivia?" I said. The little girl was around 6 years old, and had dark wavy hair and eyes like Luke – all different colors.

"I got a part in the school play. Well, you know what that means, don't you?"

"Of course. Do you want me or Luke to make the scenery?"

"I don't care. I'd love it if you both would chip in, though. Every kid at school is amazed by both of you. That would be totally rad if you guys would like make the ultimate forest scene. I can just see the other kids from other schools now." She rubbed here little hands together with glee.

I smiled. My little actress. She actually was quite good. She was in her Kindergarten play as well, and she was quite the drama queen. I had to laugh when I watched her. I had no idea where she got her theatrical nature from, but she seemed to have it since birth.

Come to think of it, she might have just a little bit of her great grandma Maggie in her. Maggie the opera singer.

I went over to hug Olivia spontaneously. "I love you, you know that?"

She rolled her eyes. "I know that. You tell me that every day."


I didn't tell her why I was always telling her how much I loved her. I didn't tell her that there was a period of time when I actually thought, several times, that she never would have been born. She probably wouldn't quite understand, nor did I want her to.


I WOKE UP WITH A START. I looked up to the sky, talking to nobody in particular. "Thank you," I said. "Thank you for helping me make the decision."

Then I pushed Luke awake. I didn't nudge him, I pushed.

He woke with a start.

"Get the doctor," I said. "Quick. Do it now. Right now."

"Okay," he said, pushing the button that signaled the doctor.

The doctor appeared within a few minutes, along with a few nurses. "Hello, Dalilah. How can I help you?"

"I need that injection. Right now. The progesterone. Right this very second."

The doctor nodded at the nurse, who left and was back in a few minutes, a syringe in her hand. "I was hoping that you would decide this." He gave me a waiver to sign, and I read it quickly and signed it.

I sighed with relief when the nurse injected me.

"This will do it, right? I'll be able to keep her, right?"

"It should," he said. "Of course, we need to do some more tests to find out why your progesterone was low. And it might be something that you're going to have to repeat until we can get that hormone up to the adequate levels. In the meantime, I recommend that you stay here in the hospital until you're out of the woods."

I nodded my head. I felt like a huge burden had been lifted off my shoulders.

After the doctor and the nurses left, I clutched Luke. "Oh, Luke, I know that this is the right decision. I know it. I'm so happy. For the first time since I found out about Olivia, I'm happy."

Luke, for his part, was grinning ear to ear. "I didn't want to pressure you into this, but this is the decision that I was praying that you would make. Secretly praying, of course."

"Praying?" I teased. "Since when do you pray?"

"Since now," he said. "What made you change your mind?"

"I saw her, Luke. And I felt...the love I had for her. I dreamed it, and the feeling that I had looking at her was incomparable. I remembered feeling that I couldn't imagine my life without her. She was beautiful in my dream – she looked like a combination of my grandmother Maggie when she was young, and you. And she was talented, already, in acting. And so intelligent. She was such a Gallagher, and also a Roberts. She was just so...us."

Luke kissed my forehead. "So us. Well, we've made a decision. We've committed."

I took another deep breath. "Yes. And I've made another decision, too. We're going to go back. We're going back, I'm getting a top lawyer, and we're going to the mattresses with Nottingham. Legally. Let the chips fall where they may. I can't have my daughter grow up with a mother who doesn't do things the right way. I need to be the person that she can look up to, and I can't do that if I continue to do stuff that is less than legal."

Luke smiled big. "Now we're talking."

"But I'm scared, Luke. I won't lie. I'm terrified of the outcome. I have to have some faith, though. My dream meant something. I hope my dream meant that it's all going to be okay. I hope and pray that's what it means."

"Oh, since when do *you* pray?" Luke teased.

"Since now."

I was dead serious.

# Chapter Eleven

I had to stay in the hospital for seven days. For seven days, Luke and I brainstormed from my hospital bed. Once my decision was made to keep Olivia, it became a matter of Luke and I putting our energies into figuring it all out.

There was so much to do, so much to figure out. Not just about getting a DNA test and hiring an aggressive lawyer. But also about what Luke and I were going to do for money once we got back. Luke finally admitted to me that he was hoping that Marcella might be a good connection for him there in London, and he asked me if I minded if he had lunch with her to pick her brain. Ask her if she knew anybody in New York who might be able to connect him to the right people again.

I told him that I was fine with that, and Luke did have lunch with her one day and came back and reported that Marcella did, in fact, know other artists who lived in the Village and had formed a co-op like they had in London. The artists all had different kinds of mediums and genres, so they all helped one another. Luke also reported that the group would be a good fit for him, according to Marcella, and he had the names and numbers of some of the artists. Marcella had assured Luke that they would welcome him with open arms.

And hopefully me, too. I had gotten out of my art during my pregnancy, just because the pregnancy and Nottingham had consumed my thoughts during that time. Composing was low on my list, unfortunately. But my mind was clearing up every day, now that I made a decision on exactly what to do, and I was happy with the decision, so I was itching to get back to my canvas. Truth be told, I wasn't happy at all about my other decisions to run and to try to blackmail Nottingham. I wasn't happy, and my gut told me that these actions weren't right. I ignored my gut, of course, and I shuddered to think that kind of disaster might have befallen me if I would have continued on with my previous course of action.

As for my posing nude, now that I was pregnant, I doubted very seriously that I would return to the nude modeling thing. Not that I wouldn't be in demand – pregnant women often were very much in demand, because many artists enjoyed painting the pregnant female form. Burgeoning breasts and bellies often made for a very sensual and voluptuous portrait.

But I wanted to get away from all of that. There was something inside of me that was just now kicking in. The maternal instinct. I suddenly wanted to leave behind all of my questionable choices and do everything right. Not that posing nude was morally questionable, of course. But I felt almost embarrassed for doing it. I didn't know why I felt embarrassed. I only knew that I did.

So, our conversations centered around the practicalities of all that Luke and I had to do when we got back to the States.

"Okay," I said. "So, I think that I should hire Marissa Herschel. Nick highly recommends her, and I liked her a lot when I went to see her. She specializes in family law, too, and I know that she knows all the major cases that are relevant here. She might look like a little petite aunt, but her reputation is solid."

Luke was nodding his head. "Okay. Well, I checked out this Steve Singleton guy. The one that Marissa said Nottingham has on permanent retainer. Aggressive isn't the word, according to the online reviews of his work. There's been a shit-ton of bar complaints against him for some of the shady stuff that he pulls, but he's gotten out of every one. It seems that he knows just where the line is as far as ethics go, and he goes right up to it, without going over it. He's a clever one, I can tell you that."

"Well, he's a bully, sounds like. Marissa might be the right person to counteract that. She's not a bully. She obviously has a different approach to litigating her cases than Steve does, and that just might do us justice. She wins a lot of her cases, too. I've been doing my own research on her cases, and I've seen some doozies that she's managed to pull off."

"As long as she can hold her own against a bully, then you might be right. I would much rather have a lawyer that knows the art of finesse than a bull in a China shop."

"Me too."

So, it was settled. Marissa Herschel would be my attorney. But I wasn't quite sure when I would be able to go back home. It would all depend on when my doctor assessed that I was out of the woods as far as my hormone levels and bed rest. I didn't call her to make an appointment from my hospital bed, although I was really itching to.

Next thing was getting a DNA test. I did my research and found out that I could get an accurate DNA test from 10 weeks on. Since I was already past that point, Luke and I got online and found a lab that could do this testing as soon as I was released from the hospital. This was crucial – I wanted to have these results as soon as possible. Not just because I wasn't 100% positive that Luke was the father, although that was a factor. I felt it in my gut that Luke was the dad, and I always had felt that way. I had no doubt that the DNA test would be affirmative in that regard.

But I couldn't be 100% sure until we actually got the test results. So, I was anxious to get that done.

I also wanted the DNA test for a very practical reason – I wanted my ducks lined up before I set foot on United States' soil.

On and on and on Luke and I talked, the entire time that I laid in that hospital bed. It felt wonderful, because we were bonding again. I was starting to feel that there was a barrier between him and I ever since I was pregnant, and I worried about that. I had secretly worried that perhaps Luke wasn't happy about the pregnancy.

But it wasn't that at all. Luke just wasn't happy with my ideas about handling the pregnancy and handling Nottingham. Once I decided to do things the right way, the tension had disappeared.

We were best friends again, and I still felt that spark of electricity every time he touched me. The tingle of excitement.

And my hormones were going wild. I realized, several times during that week, that I wanted him in the worst way possible. If only the doctor would give me the green light, I know that I would have ripped off his clothes and have him fuck me right there in that hospital bed. And why not? It was a private room, courtesy of the wealthy Liam.

But I knew that I couldn't risk anything going wrong, just because I let my lust for Luke get the best of me.

# Chapter Twelve

I finally was released from the hospital. My hormone levels were finally in check. The doctor did caution me that I might have a chance of a difficult pregnancy, so I needed to be diligent about my prenatal checkups. More diligent than most women, he cautioned.

"Of course," I said. "I wouldn't do anything to jeopardize this pregnancy for the world at this point."

And, the first thing that we did was arrange for the DNA test to occur right there in that same hospital. I gave some blood and Luke gave a hair sample. I had already spoken with a counselor about this occurring, so it was just a matter of giving the samples to the lab and the results would be available in just over a week.

I was nervous about that, but not really. I had learned, long ago, to trust my gut. Which was why it was so embarrassing to realize that I had almost done something really stupid and against my gut instinct in trying to blackmail Nottingham instead of fighting him fair and square.

My gut was screaming that Luke was the father, and it always had been.

Liam sent a limo to pick me up on the day that I was released, as he was working that day.

While I sat in the back of the limo, I made an appointment with Marissa to come in the following week. Again, I needed my ducks in a row. With my DNA test and Marissa on retainer, I knew that I had a fighting chance.

The issue of my paying for Marissa, of course, was still up in the air. Luke insisted on using the leftover money from his show to pay the retainer. I was just as insistent that I was going to use my father's money to pay. We needed to live on the rest of Luke's money, which was just over $50,000 by then, after he took out money for his taxes and he had paid for most of the expenses that we incurred while staying with Liam.

Little did I know that this soon wouldn't even be as much of an issue.

WHEN LUKE AND I ARRIVED AT LIAM'S, to my surprise, Neil and the other Pixxallators was sitting in the kitchen with their instruments in hand. Liam grinned and came up to me, putting his arm around me. "Lass, you're home. You're looking well, too."

"I feel well, thanks so much," I said. Then I looked at the boys and back to Liam questioningly.

"Ah, well, this is a surprise for you and Luke." Liam was smiling broadly. He looked almost mischievous.

"I'm sorry," I said. "I don't understand." I felt uncomfortable seeing Neil again. For his part, he looked mildly embarrassed. After all, he was pretty drunk the last time I saw him and he was so blunt about what he wanted with me.

Liam just smiled and said to the boys "hit it."

They did, and Luke immediately recognized the song. "Hey, that's one of mine." He looked astonished. "I mean, I have to admit that the arrangement is slightly different then the way that I wrote it, but it sounds pretty cool nonetheless."

My heart soared. Did this mean that the boys wanted to record one of Luke's songs? It was a cool song, too. The lyrics rang of heartbreak and despair, and I surmised that this might have been one of the songs that Luke composed after we broke up. The arrangement was different than what I had imagined for one of Luke's songs, too, as I had listened to Luke's songs, and he almost a grungy sound. This arrangement was airy and light, despite the dark lyrics, and it definitely reminded me of something that would have been recorded in the early 1980s by Tears for Fears or something. Other parts of the song echoed the lush vibe of 311.

After they were done with the song, Liam just smiled at me. "Lass, I wanted to surprise you." He turned to Luke. "I've been listening to your songs, mate. You've got a lot of talent. I also think that the Pixxallators would be perfect for at least three of your songs. Let's talk terms."

Luke still looked just a bit shocked. He had no idea that I had given Liam his songs. I never told him, as I was afraid that Liam wouldn't like them, and I didn't want Luke's feelings to be hurt if that were the case.

Finally, Luke shook his head. "Uh, yeah, yeah, sure. I'm just surprised. I mean, I've thought about asking you about listening to some of my songs, but I was too embarrassed." He looked at me and smiled. "But sounds like Dalilah didn't have the same compunction. Lucky me."

So, Luke and Liam went into the library, presumably to talk about drawing up a contract.

Neil, for his part, came up to me. "I'm sorry about being so rude the other night, Dalilah. It was the liquor talking, I promise you."

"Not at all," I said. "You guys did a great job with Luke's song."

"We've practiced some of his other ones as well. I think that they have potential. Would you like to hear them?"

"I'd love to," I said.

So, the boys played three other songs. I was surprised at the range. One was more of a ballad, but the boys put their own special touch with it. I smiled as I listened to the lyrics, imagining that Luke wrote this song with me in mind. The other two were more up-tempo, and I could definitely hear Luke's words in them. They were heart-felt, even with the peppier arrangements.

I loved all of them.

About an hour later, Luke and Liam came out of the library. Both men looked happy.

"Dalilah," he said. "I have to have this agreement looked over by an attorney, of course, but it sounds like a good one. Liam has offered me $15,000 for my four songs, plus royalties if the boys decide to record them. That could really add up, although I have to admit that I'm naïve when it comes to this sort of thing. I never imagined that my songs would sell, so I never imagined that I would be in this position." Luke then went into the intricacies of the proposed contract, talking about how much he would get every time the boys performed the songs in concert verses how much he would get from the recorded versions of the songs, and how all of that would be calculated.

I listened, interested. "So, if any one of these songs is a hit, then that could add up to a lot of money, huh?"

"It could," he said. "But the up-front would be really helpful. That's another $15,000 that we can put towards your legal fees."

I sighed. "Luke, I-"

"Nope. I'm going to take care of you, Dalilah. That's what men do. Your dad doesn't have to get involved at all. You and I can get a place together, we'll watch our pennies, and we'll make this all work out. I got art, and, once you start creating, too, we'll both be bringing in a good income. In the meantime, we have this money from Liam, assuming that I agree to these terms, plus the leftover money from my show, and some good leads from Marcella on making more money from my art. We'll make this work, Dalilah. You and me."

At that moment, I didn't think that I could love a man more.

# Chapter Thirteen

That night, after the boys left the house, and all of us had dinner out in the sun porch, Luke and I went up to our room. It was really the first time that I had been in that room and not felt a sense of foreboding or urgency. A sense of stress and tension. All of that was gone, and, for right at that moment, I felt a sense of calm. Of peace. I had made my decision, and, although I knew that it was far from a slam dunk – about as far from a slam dunk as could possibly be – just the fact that I had a course of action made me feel like I was finally in control of the situation.

So, I was finally ready to concentrate on other things. Mainly Luke. And how I was feeling about him. He was showing himself to be the man that I had always wanted – strong, protective, with a good sense of ethics. I loved that he stood up to me when I was going to go down the wrong path, and I loved that he was so willing to make sure that he and I were a team in this endeavor. He wasn't about to make me twist in the wind, so to speak. He was going to be right there.

I laid down on the bed, and he laid down next to me. Both of us were really exhausted from the whirlwind few weeks that we had spent in London. But that didn't really matter, right at that moment. Because we had each other, and I was feeling so horny right then, I just couldn't stand it any longer.

He put his hand in my hair, and kissed my forehead, his eyes closed. I closed my eyes, too, and breathed in his scent of faint cologne and man. "Things are going to be okay, Dalilah," he said. "I'll make sure of it."

And I knew that he would. I felt safe and protected right at that moment, and that feeling, combined with the knowledge that Luke was going to be an amazing father, was enough to make me feel pure intoxication. "I know, Luke. I know that now."

I didn't want to talk about all that, though. What was ahead of us wasn't on my mind right at that moment. What was on my mind was a sense of pure animal lust. As Luke gently ran his hand along my arm, causing all of my hairs to stand on end, I sighed. My breath was already starting to become heavy, as he gently touched me.

Then he started kissing me. Gently at first, then more insistent. His lips were drinking in mine, while he left hand was on my cheek, stroking it gently. I put his hand on my crotch, and he stroked it through my jeans. He lay on top of me, and I could feel his erection standing at attention through his own pants. He gently thrust against me as he continued to kiss me.

Then he started stroking my stomach, and he deftly detached my bra with one flick of his finger. He ran his hand on my swelling breast, and lightly fingered my nipple. His finger swirled around the nipple while he continued to gently thrust into me through his jeans. I bucked up a little, my wetness meeting his hardness, and then I put my hand in my pants and fingered myself. I was soaking wet at that point, so I put my finger inside of myself, and groaned with pure pleasure.

Luke looked at me. "I have to say that I'm nervous. I don't want anything to happen to the little one."

"Nothing will, I promise. I'm out of the woods, and the doctor said that I could do this. In fact, he encouraged me to. Please fuck me."

"You don't have to ask twice," he said with a smile.

Then he put his own finger in my wet pussy, and swirled it around inside. I groaned as he also put his thumb on my clit, and rubbed it gently. He kissed my neck, and pulled off my top. While one of his hands was gently fingering me, the other hand was stroking my breast. His lips were soon on my breasts, and I groaned again as I felt him gently stroking my nipple with his tongue, and nibbling on each of my nipples. I reached down and felt my wetness, and my hand covered his.

He started to work his way down my belly with his tongue and lips, and then his head was between my legs. I wrapped my ankles behind his neck, and he pulled off my jeans and panties. I flexed my feet in pleasure as he worked his tongue around my clit and inside of me, while his fingers explored my rear opening. I bucked up, feeling my entire body break out in goose pimples. A flush and warm sensation coursed throughout my skin, and my blood started pumping hard.

While his fingers continued to explore my ass, he worked his way down, kissing my inner thigh and nibbling it a tiny bit. He massaged my clit with his free hand, sending a burning sensation throughout my lower region. He pulsed his fingers in and out of my pussy, and gently tugged on my pussy lips. Then he was kissing my stomach again, making his way up to my breasts. He kissed both of my breasts, and then kissed my lips, running his hands through my hair.

I put my hand on his manhood, which was pitching a tent through his pants. He unbuttoned his pants and kicked them off, and I tore off his boxer-briefs. I flipped him over, and started kissing his neck, and I bit each of his nipples, before I went lower. I gently licked the head of his erection, and he moaned and thrust a little bit into my mouth. I put my hand on the bottom of his shaft, as my lips worked up and down, in rhythm with my hand. I gently squeezed his balls, and licked his opening, before returning my mouth to his enormous erection.

"Oh, god, Dalilah, that feels amazing," he said, but then flipped me over on my back. "But I have to be inside of you right now."

I nodded my head. I hadn't wanted anything, ever, as much as I wanted him inside of me at that moment. Ever.

So, by the time he finally thrusted inside of me, I was already on fire. He filled me up, slowly, inch by inch, and I screamed in pleasure. He pulled on my hair, and kissed my breasts while he slowly but surely thrust in and out. I turned my head, and he kissed my neck and nibbled on my ear. I put my hands over my head, and he gripped them behind me.

My breathing and heartbeat were so fast during this time that I started to feel just a little bit light-headed. I finally inhaled a sharp breath, and scratched my nails into his back. I turned him over on his back, and started to ride him hard. I ducked my head, and kissed him eagerly. He then turned me around, and entered me from behind. I groaned as I came to orgasm, one so powerful that it felt like the earth was opening up. I felt his hot cum squirt inside of me, and I let out an enormous breath.

He remained behind me, his hand on one of my breasts. He kissed the back of my neck gently. "Mmmm, Dalilah. That was amazing. As usual."

"Oh, it certainly was," I said, feeling my legs trembling as he ran his hands on them. "It always is, though."

"I feel so connected to you now. Like there isn't anything between us. There's nothing that we can't do, as long as we do it together." He kissed me gently on my mouth, and I groaned.

I flipped him over on his back again. "You might as well know, now that I'm pregnant, I'm going to probably wear you out. Maybe I should try to have you cloned so that I can fuck you all the time."

Luke just laughed. "No need for there to be a clone. I think that I can handle you all on my own."

"You think?" I asked, as I took his flaccid penis in my hand, and tugged on it. It started to grow, and I sat down on top of him again. I put my hand on his shoulders, and rode him until his hot cum squirted inside of me again.

Luke was breathing hard. "Yes, I think," he said, kissing me.

"You like a challenge, do you?" I asked.

"Love a challenge."

I smiled. I wondered if he really knew what he was getting into. But, as he started kissing me, and stroking my thigh, before thrusting into me again, I knew that he would be up for the challenge.


WE FINALLY GOT SOME SLEEP, and, when I woke up the next day, I stretched and looked out the window. It was another sunny, peaceful day. A bird landed on the terrace, and I felt just a little bit charmed by the little creature. I started to feel sad that we would be leaving this bucolic setting. I wasn't even quite sure where we would land when we got back to New York City. I knew that we couldn't live with my parents or with Nick, as they both lived in the suburbs. I, for one, wanted to be in the city. I wanted to be close to the action, and, hopefully, close to where Luke's new artists' co-op was. I also thought that I should be close by where my new lawyer was, as well as the courthouses.

The problem was that my apartment was sub-leased, and Luke had moved out of his. This was the arrangement that we both made when we came out to London. I hated to kick out the girl who was subletting my place, but I knew that I could, as I never actually made a binding contract with her. Still, it was in the middle of the month, so I couldn't just land in New York and tell her to get out. That wouldn't be right.

That was the last piece of the puzzle, really. I wanted to leave as soon as possible. I wanted to get after it. Luke did, too. Not that Liam wasn't helpful and welcoming, because he certainly was. His house was gorgeous, and this bed was completely comfortable. I loved the terrace and I adored all the nature that surrounded his place.

But it was time to leave.

I knew that there was one place where Luke and I could go. And I was more than prepared for his objections.

"Luke," I said. "We have to make plans to leave. We've talked about everything but where we're going to stay when we get back. I don't think that I can just kick out my sub-lessor in the middle of the month. You don't have your apartment any more. We can't stay with my parents, because they live several hours a way. Nick is out in Connecticut." I took a deep breath. "But Serena lives in the Village. She has a large, beautiful brownstone there. Three bedrooms, hardwood floors, crown moldings. It's in a pre-war building." I felt like a real estate agent as I described the rest of her place.

"How do you know so much about Serena's place?" Luke asked me. I felt a little bit encouraged that he didn't automatically say "no," but, rather, led off with something more neutral.

I shrugged. "She showed me pictures when I had dinner with her. I asked her about her place, because I was curious. Anyhow, it looks pretty awesome inside. She said that it's in an upscale neighborhood there in the Village, with trees lining the streets. It sounds like heaven, really."

Luke looked at the ceiling briefly and scrunched up his face. "Are you sure that she would be okay with us staying with her temporarily? I mean, she and I have never gotten along. Although I will have to say that I'm still grateful to her for what she did for me in the Nottingham situation."

I felt even more encouraged. I was prepared for Luke to say that we would stay with Serena over his dead body. But it did sound like it was something that he would actually consider.

"I'm not sure," I said. "That she will be willing to have us stay with her. But that would be perfect, wouldn't it? Your artists co-op is in the Village, and being in that vibe would be so helpful for both of us. I would be totally excited to live there with her, even temporarily. I really hope that I could get into that co-op as well."

Luke stroked his chin. "Well, it's a thought. Although I hate having to impose on all these people. First Liam, now Serena maybe. I personally can't wait until there comes a time when you and I just have our own place. Just you and me. That will hopefully be sooner than you might think. At any rate, I think that by the time Olivia arrives, we're going to have to have our own place. So, I better get moving with my art."

"Well, okay, then. I know what you mean as far as imposing on others, and you're right – I hope that there will come a time when we don't have to. But, for now, it seems like the best choice for us. Assuming that she doesn't mind, of course."

Luke just grimaced. "Let's go downstairs and see if Liam is expecting us for breakfast, and then we'll have to figure it out from there, I guess. One thing's for sure, we need to make a decision soon."

# Chapter Fourteen

## LUKE

I somehow knew that Dalilah was going to want us to stay with Serena. A few months ago, I would have howled in protest, no matter how much Dalilah liked the woman. But, when she helped me with my assault issue, I saw a different side to her. She didn't have to help me like that, and she really stuck out her neck, too. That entire thing could have gone way south, and she would have been put into jail alongside me. She was gutsy for doing that, and she really saved my bacon.

So, I had mixed feelings when Dalilah brought up to me that she wanted to try to stay with Serena. On one hand, I knew that Serena's place would be perfect, if it was as nice as Dalilah said that it was. I had always wanted to live in the Village, because I craved being around that kind of atmosphere. Being around other artists, and writers, poets, actors and all types of creative people would be the absolute best scenario. I had to admit that my place in Brooklyn was not exactly conducive to composing my best.

On the other hand, I still didn't 100% trust Serena. As much as I knew that she was trying to change, I felt that it might be too hard for her to completely change enough. It might be a matter of time until the old Serena comes out, and she and I would be at each other's throats. I no longer felt that Serena was bad to the core. I now knew that she wasn't, and that, inwardly, she was really a good person. But I didn't entirely think that her behavior would change drastically. And, if Dalilah and I lived with her, all of that would have to come out. If she was still a liar and a manipulator, there would be no covering that up if we were there 24/7.

*Well, hopefully we don't necessarily have to stay there for very long.* Dalilah was just going to have to kick out her sub-lessee, but I understood that Dalilah was probably hesitant to ask the girl to leave until she could find a new place.

We made a mess, Dalilah and me, by hastily coming out here to London in the first place. Now, it was time to clean it up.

So, Dalilah and I had to figure it all out. We had breakfast with Liam, which consisted of croissants and eggs, with a side of strawberry pots de crème, which was basically strawberry pudding.

"Well, Liam," Dalilah said. "You've been awesome, letting us stay here. It was just what I needed, to come here and try to figure out what was going on and what I needed to do. But we think that it might be time to go home and fight."

Liam smiled. "Ah, so you aren't going to try your blackmail scheme, huh? Too bad. I probably could have helped you with that."

"Nah," Dalilah said. "I decided that I needed to do things the right way. Otherwise, I don't know that I could wake up every morning and look at myself in the mirror."

"So, when are you leaving?" Liam asked.

"Within the week," Dalilah said. "We just have to tie up some loose ends." *Like where we're going to stay.*

"Okay, then," Liam said. "I'm going to miss you and Luke. I felt like we were just getting to know each other."

"I know." Dalilah smiled, and gripped my hand. I nodded.

I knew that the loose end that Dalilah was talking about involved my sister. I felt apprehensive, but, at the same time, I knew that it had to be done.

So, after breakfast, Dalilah and I went to our room. I picked up the phone, and dialed Serena's number.

"Luke," she said, picking it up. "Long time, no hear."

"I know," I said. "I've been, uh, busy."

"Huh. Busy."

Somehow, I thought that Serena probably knew exactly what was going on. She always seemed to, it seemed.

"Yes," I said, suddenly feeling uncomfortable. "Well, as you know, Dalilah is pregnant. I'm sure that you also know the dilemma that she's been in with that. I mean, considering the fact that she's currently married to Nottingham and all."

"Of course," she said. "That certainly is a situation, isn't it?"

"Yes," I said. "Well, here's what happened." I then launched into how Dalilah and I decided to run to London to try to figure things out, and how we ultimately decided to come back to New York to try to work it out with a lawyer.

"And you need a place to stay," she said. "I got it."

"Yes," I said, squeezing my eyes shut. I was prepared for her to say "no," which would mean that Dalilah and I would have to go back to the drawing board after all.

"Okay," she said. "I've got plenty of room here, and, to be honest, it's been just a little bit lonely here. It might be kind of nice to have people around here."

I let out my breath. I wasn't entirely sure that I was happy that Serena agreed to let us live with her so quickly, or if I was apprehensive. A part of me actually wished that she would say no, and Dalilah and I would have to figure something else out for the time being.

"Well, thank you. Dalilah and I are leaving here in a few days. I hope that's not too short of notice. She really wants to get rolling with this custody situation. Get her ducks in a row before she faces down Nottingham."

"No, not too short of notice at all. Just let me know when I can expect you guys, and I'll be there at the airport to pick you up."

I looked at Dalilah, who was looking at me expectantly. I gave her the thumb's up, and she looked relieved.

"Okay," I said. "Well, thanks again. I mean, we won't have to stay with you too very long. Just until Dalilah can kick out her sub-lessee."

"However much time you need," Serena said. "I'll talk to you soon, huh?"

"Soon." And I hung up.

"So, it's all set?" Dalilah asked me. "Serena is okay with us staying with her and everything?"

"Yeah," I said. "It seems like it. She said that she's lonely there, anyhow, so it sounds like she might actually be looking forward to it, to be honest with you."

"Awesome," Dalilah said. "Well, let's get some plane tickets, and let's go home."

I knew that it went without saying that Dalilah wasn't going to call her dad to send his plane.

So, I clicked online, bought two one-way tickets to La Guardia.

We soon would be going home.

# Chapter Fifteen
## DALILAH

On the plane on the way home, it was time for decompress. I was feeling just a little bit airsick, so I made sure that I had a bag close. Luke got us First Class tickets, so I was comfortable enough. But I was more than a little sad to be leaving Liam's gorgeous house, and I was extremely apprehensive about going to war with Nottingham.

One thing that was nice was that Luke and I got the DNA test results back early. It confirmed what I knew all along – that Luke was the father of the baby. That brought both of us a lot of joy, of course. And it made both of us more determined than ever to fight to the death to make sure that Nottingham would never get a chance to get his hands on this child.

Luke gripped my hand. The air hostess came around and took our order. This airline was offering a variety of sandwiches, chips and drinks. I ordered a veggie sandwich with chips, and Luke ordered a burger. I also wanted a tomato juice, and Luke got orange juice.

As always, Luke all but read my mind. "You're scared. I know you are. But you have to have some faith. Have some faith in the legal system, and have some faith in the universe. Everything is going to turn out just the way that it should."

"I hope you're right. I really do."

"I am. Not that I have a magic crystal ball, but I do think that everything is going to work in our favor."

The food came, but I picked at it a little. Luke nudged me. "I know that you really don't feel like it, but you have to at least try to eat. You might actually feel a bit better if you do."

I shook my head. "I know that you're right, but it's always been difficult for me to try to force food on myself if I just not feeling up to it. But I'll try."

I nibbled on the sandwich, and put a few chips into my mouth. The salt on my tongue tasted good, so I delved into the bag of chips a bit more. Before I knew it, I had demolished the bag of chips and I started in on the sandwich. When I polished that off, I knew that Luke was right. I *was* feeling better.

After I ate, I put my head on Luke's shoulder. I knew that this was going to be a long plane ride, but the comfort of his shoulder made me feel like it wasn't going to be that terrible.


THE PLANE FINALLY LANDED. I was proud that I got through the trip back across the pond without puking once. Luke and I walked through the security part of the airport and headed for the baggage claim.

Serena was waiting for us by the baggage claim. She came up to me, and put her arm around me. "How you feeling, Dalilah?" she asked. "God, you guys have had a time of it, haven't you?"

"You have no idea."

She then went over to Luke and gave him a hug. "Good to see you, kid. And how are you holding up?"

"Been better," he said. "Thanks again for taking us in."

Serena nodded. "To tell you the truth, I was happy that you called and more than happy that you wanted to come and stay with me." She didn't elaborate on that, though.

Luke and I got our bags, and Serena helped us by taking some of our baggage. We all walked to her Lexus, and she put the bags in the trunk. I sat up front, and Luke sat in the back.

"Now," she said. "You're going to have to explain things just a little bit more. What is going on with your child and Nottingham? I mean, you did a DNA test, right?"

"Right," I said. "And Luke is definitely the father."

"Ah," she said, looking in her rear-view mirror at Luke. "I have some Cuban cigars at home for you." She smiled. "Don't ask me where I got them, either. I'll never tell. But go on."

"Well, because I'm married to Nottingham, and, well, at the time that I conceived, I had been living with Nottingham just a few days prior, the law says that Nottingham is presumed the father."

"Tell me what I'm missing," Serena said. "You get a judge, you show them the DNA test that Nottingham isn't the dad, and everybody walks away with a smile. Right?"

"Well, it isn't as easy as all of that, unfortunately. There are some judges who won't even allow DNA evidence into the courtroom if the presumed father challenges the right to the child. There are others who might allow it, but then still rule that Nottingham has rights. It all depends on the best interest of the child. So, it's a crap shoot, really."

"And what makes you even think that Nottingham is going to challenge this? He might just decide that he wants no part in it."

"He might," I said. "But I know him. Any chance at all to get at me, he's going to take. I mean, look at the lengths that he went to put Luke into prison. And what could devastate me more than getting his corrupt hands on my child?"

"True that," she said. "Well, I'm sorry to hear about all you guys are going through, but I'm happy to help with anything that you might need." Then she looked at Luke. "You need money, kid? Those lawyer types can get pretty expensive. I speak from experience, there."

"No," Luke said. "We're okay. But, if you were going to offer, I thank you."

She shrugged. "I was going to offer, but I understand if you don't want to feel like you owe me. But I'm your big sis. I know that I haven't always been there for you, because, well, I've been kind of a bitch all these years. I'm here for you now, though."

In spite of himself, Luke smiled and then laughed. "Sorry, Serena, I don't mean to laugh. It was just the way that you came out with that statement about you being a bitch. It was kinda funny the way that you said it."

Serena laughed too. "Yeah? Well, I'm glad that you find me humorous, instead of hating me. Maybe you can talk to dad, Chris, Mark and Amy too, huh? I would like to be welcomed back into the family, as opposed to feeling like such a pariah all the time."

"I'll be sure to do that," Luke said, honestly.

We drove along until we got into a tree-lined street of brownstones. There were kids playing on the sidewalk and women walking their dogs. One of them stopped to talk to Serena, and I was kinda amazed about how much Serena seemed to love the dogs. Every time we got to one, she would bend down and baby-talk the animals, and she let every one of them lick her face.

I was charmed by this, really. I always was partial to people who loved animals. I always wished that I had the passion to really commit to animal welfare, like my parents. They really walked the walk. Neither of them used any animal products, at all – they wouldn't even make Jell-O for me when I was growing up, because it was made with animal products. Lanolin was strictly verboten because it was made from sheep. I knew that even they were not always that way – before they got involved with their animal sanctuary, they ate meat and used animal products.

But I never could commit. I always wanted to, but, somehow peer pressure always got the best of me. It had something to do with my desire to be normal, and I never was because of my abilities. So, I needed something to make me feel like I wasn't such a freak, so I went along with everyone else and indulged in animal products.

I wondered how Serena felt about all of that. Come to think about it, I had never seen her eat any kind of animal product. Even during the Christmas dinner, she didn't partake in the turkey. She just made a plate of the trimmings and didn't make a big deal of it.

We eventually followed Serena into her home. Her home was a two-level place with hardwood floors throughout, and crown moldings. A bay window was in the living room, with throw pillows on the ledge. Her kitchen was enormous, by New York City standards, as it was large enough to have an island in the middle. Her countertops were dark blue granite, and her appliances were all new, including her gas burners. Throughout the home there were houseplants and real trees.

In all, it was a cozy home, yet, by the standards that I was used to in New York, it seemed like a veritable mansion.

"You know," I said to her. "I never even asked you this. And I don't think that Luke was very clear, either. What is it that you do?"

She smiled. "I was a law partner at a firm here in town. But we didn't do family law, so I can't really help you there. We were more into white-collar defense, so, you know, we got paid the big bucks. We also defended pharmaceutical companies." She paused. "I got out of that, though, and I got money now because, well, I hate to admit it, but my ex-husband is pretty wealthy." Her eyes gleamed. "And, what can I say, I know a lot about him. A little too much for his comfort. Which means that I was able to extract a pretty good settlement from him. Now, well, I'm trying to find myself."

I nodded. I kinda knew what she meant by that. "Trying to find yourself. God, that sounds so familiar."

"Does it?" she asked. "Well, Dalilah, it's one thing to try to figure it all out when you're only 20 years old and haven't really lived. It's quite another when you're 28, gone through college, gone through law school, been married, etc. I should have more figured out than I do. You – well, when you're 20, you're not supposed to know crap. So don't feel bad."

"But," I said, and then whispered. "You're just now trying to come to terms with what happened to you when you were a baby. That's why you're having problems right now."

Serena looked over at Luke, who was examining a picture that she had on her wall. He was apparently oblivious to Serena and me talking, as he examined the shapes and colors that were on the canvas in front of him. That was Luke – sometimes, he could get so lost in a piece of art, he barely knew that he had surroundings at all. "Yes," she said. "That's true. Listen, Luke doesn't know about all of that. I hope you haven't told him."

"I haven't," I said. "You told me not to, and I'm going to be as good as my word."

"Thanks," she said. "I mean, I probably should tell him sometime about it, but I'm afraid that he's going to freak out. I mean, he had that same baby-sitter. I wonder if she did anything to him when he was a kid? I mean, probably not. One thing about Luke, he's always been a great kid. Always. Man, sometimes I so much wanted to be like him. Trade places with him. He has always seemed like somebody who not only rolls with the punches, but shakes off the pain of all that has happened to him. When I see Chris, I know what Luke could have turned out like if things would have gone a different way for him. But I'm so glad that it didn't."

"Why? What's up with Chris?"

"Egads. Drugs, cutting, you name it. But Chris was a special case. He saw our mom die. Our mom died trying to save him. That has to fuck up a person, no matter what."

I nodded my head. "Yeah," I said. "Sometimes I think that perhaps what happened to me when I was a baby affected me."

Serena looked at me wisely, as if she knew what had happened with Andrew and my dad. "I suspected as much. You've known darkness. I mean, I know that Luke has told me about how criticism made you turn against yourself, but I always thought that there was something more."

"There was. When I was a baby, I was so afraid that my dad was going to die. I couldn't even put it into words. I was a young child, yet I knew that there were things that were seriously wrong. My dad was shot, he almost died, and I was always afraid that he would just not wake up one day. And, well, I think that I always carried around the fear that I almost died, too, when this crazed gun-man had me."

I then launched into the story of Andrew, my father and my mother. "Well, that explains it," she said, taking my hand. "Perhaps that was why your art was always so deep. So dark. You know, I've looked at your stuff on-line. It amazed me that you were only 11, not just because you had the ability to do what you did, but also because you had the experience to produce that stuff. Those raw, explosive paintings. They came from somewhere. They weren't the work of a girl who hadn't known tragedy."

I smiled. Perhaps Serena was right. I had never even thought about what kind of hurt and rage was bubbling beneath the surface when I composed that stuff. "Yes, I suppose you're right. And that was probably why I became so depressed when I lost my voice and my abilities. Because I no longer had an outlet for what I was feeling. Not just about that stuff about my dad almost dying, and me being in the arms of a crazy man. But also because I have never felt like I have fit in. As much as I've always wanted to be normal, it was very difficult for me. And I think that my art always reflected that."

Serena nodded her head. "That was what I saw, too, when I looked at your paintings. Someone who was really like me. Because I never fit in, either. I always had the special sight that made me feel that I was weird. The ability to see things and know things which others couldn't. I mean, there was a spirit who befriended me when I was 11. And my dad would come into the room when I was talking to Thomas. That was his earthly name. He didn't understand. He scolded me, and told me that I was too old for imaginary friends. So, I tried to tell Thomas to go away, but he wouldn't. And, goddamn it, I really didn't want him to. He understood me, more than anybody in my family ever did."

I smiled, and put my arm around her. "Ah, we're two freaks, aren't we? Nobody would ever know by looking at us, though." I looked over at Luke, who was at another of Serena's paintings, carefully examining it. "I wonder if Luke has ever felt like that. Ostracized, like an outcast. He's such a good-natured, gorgeous guy. I doubt that he has ever felt like that."

"Well," Serena said. "Maybe not to the extent that we have. But, come on, if he's human, then he's felt moments of being weird and less-than. I'm quite sure. If he hasn't, then he's the weird one, not us."

"True," I said.

THAT EVENING, WHILE SERENA AND LUKE shared a bottle of wine, and I enjoyed some Perrier, we discussed what was going to happen in the morning. "I have an appointment with Marissa Herschel in the morning. And, from there, I'm going to file for divorce and see what shakes out."

"Are you scared?" Serena asked me.

"Are you kidding me? I'm petrified. It's bad enough that I have to ask for a divorce at all, but to admit that I'm pregnant…the knives are going to come out, I can guarantee you this."

"Yeah, well, just have guts. You wouldn't believe some of the stuff that I've come out of. I'll have to tell you some of my exploits later on. But I always had faith that the universe knows what the fuck it's doing."

Luke was sitting next to me, drinking his wine, and playing absent-mindedly with my neck. "That's what I'm counting on. We're finally going to draw our inside straight, and we're going to not only beat this down, fair and square, but we're going to come out of it happy. I'd like to think that, in the battle of good verses evil, the good should win. Although I know that's not always the case."

"Oh, I wish that I could be so optimistic," Serena said. "Not to mention naïve." She shook her head. "But you have to know that I've not always been on the side of the angels. My old law firm handled cases where the people were as crooked and base as they come. Unfortunately, we were good at what we did, so these unbelievable bastards would just walk away. These greedy fucks would embezzle millions, or get caught doing all kinds of blatant acts of fraud, or cheated people out of millions of dollars, and they'd either walk or pay a small penalty for it. Thanks to us."

She shook her head. "Never underestimate human nature, kid. There's a part of every one of us that isn't so nice. We might acknowledge it, or we might not. But it's always there. And, sometimes, people who display their dark side for all the world to see, gets away with it. Just sayin."

I was quiet. I knew that she was right. Having been in the world of the privileged and the high society, I knew, first-hand, how people could be when it came to money. To maintaining a certain image and lifestyle. Those were the people who Serena defended in her old job. That was Nottingham. Nottingham was a zero-sum guy, too. He had to be. Nobody could be as wealthy as he was, at such a young age, without stepping on more than one toe along the way. He knew how to play dirty.

And something told me that playing dirty was exactly what he was going to do with me.

# Chapter Sixteen

## LUKE

After dinner, Dalilah and I decided that we needed a shower. So, we headed up to our private bathroom, which was attached to the bedroom where we were staying, and climbed on in.

This was a time for us to relax and just enjoy each other. Tomorrow would be a stressful day for her, I knew, so I wanted to have this evening just to be with her. To let he know how much I loved her, and how much I would always be there for her. No matter what.

She took off her clothes to join me in the shower. She was so beautiful, always, but, at this point, she was even more than that. She was radiant. She might have been a little bit self-conscious about her tiny little pooch, which was growing by the day, and the way that her already-ample breasts were swelling, but, I had to admit, I was completely turned on by her new body. She was sensuous. She glowed from within. The combination of her milky white skin with her red hair, and pregnancy glow and pregnancy body – there were no words to describe how hungry I was for her.

And, lucky me, she had informed me that, because of her raging hormones, she wanted to attack me every second. Since I was feeling just the same way about her, I thought that we would be a match made in heaven.

So, when both of us got into the shower, and I started to soap up her naked body, I immediately got a hard-on.

She smiled. "What's up with that?" she asked, gesturing to my boner. "I haven't even touched you yet."

"Oh, you don't have to," I said. "I only need to look at you, and I've got a hard-on. But being close to you naked like this...*mon dieu*." At that, I kissed her, and she lost her breath.

She smiled after my kiss. "Really? I mean, I'm so fat these days. I just can't stand it."

"Fat? Hardly. Voluptuous. Sensuous. Radiant. Gorgeous. Those are all good words for you. Fat never even comes to my mind, not even for a millisecond."

She sighed. "Oh, Luke. Just shut up and fuck me, would you please?"

At that, she got down on her hands and knees, and I turned off the shower. I teased her just a little by bringing down a loofah, and scrubbing her back with it. She lowered her head and moaned a little. "That feels awesome, Luke, but you know what I want. What I need. Give it to me, please."

It wasn't difficult for me to do just that. I thrust into her, and she was completely wet inside, so I was able to slip into her easily. She felt incredible, as always. She moaned loudly, as I thrust in and out of her easily yet slowly. I grabbed her beautiful breasts, and squeezed them. She moaned louder, and I thrust into her harder and harder. Then she laid down on her back, and put her legs up in the air, and I thrust into her some more.

"Give it to me, Luke. Give it to me hard. Fuck me, Luke. Goddamn, you feel so amazing."

She felt even more amazing. I tried to stop it, but I could feel my river of cum sliding inside of her. "Oh, god, I'm so sorry that was quick," I said. "You just don't know what you do to me. What you've always done to me. Being with you...I can't even describe it. It's so fucking amazing, I just can't even put it into words."

For her part, she was breathing heavily. She was still lying on the tile floor, her legs up in the air. She was shaking all over. She shook her head. "Oh, please. I know exactly what I do to you. Because you do the same to me. You know just what to do to make me go absolutely crazy with lust and desire."

At that, she flipped me over and got on top of me. She had the loofah in her hand. She scrubbed my stomach with it, and then got some oil, and rubbed it all over my chest. I groaned as she bit my neck, and then went down to my cock and started to suck it. I grabbed her hair, and brought her up to me so that I could kiss her. She met my lips with her own greedy ones, and the two of us devoured each other while she continued to massage my cock.

She smiled as she felt me getting hard again. "Hmmmm, well, maybe I can take control this time." At that, she lowered herself down on me, and the sensation was so intense, I thought that I was going to cum right then and there. But I held off, and she raised herself up so that she was at the tip of my dick, and then slammed herself down, forcefully, back on me.

I shook my head, feeling that this was sensation was more powerful than anything I had ever had before. I shuddered, trying hard to think of something, anything, that would delay the inevitable. I kissed her, as she rode me, again and again. She kept up the cadence – she almost would pull completely out, not quite, then she would slam herself down on me. Before long, though, she was more rhythmic, and she was able to squat on me rapidly. I sighed, no longer able to hold it back, and I cum inside her again.

She smiled. "Oh, see, I can get you going twice in a row."

"Do you feel powerful, Dalilah? Because you know that I'm just putty in your hands."

"Powerful isn't really the word. I would like to say that I feel sated, but I just can't, right now. I'm kind of a raging beast, I'm ashamed to say. I've never quite felt like this."

"Well, I'm more than happy to oblige," I said.

"Are you?" she said. She looked serious this time. "God, Luke, I'm just so happy, you can't imagine. I mean, everything is fucked up, of course. Everything is up in the air. But I love you so much I can't stand it." There were tears in her eyes. "I mean, everything that has happened...well, everything I did was because of my warped view of what I thought that you needed. It was all so stupid, though. But I now know that, really, you just need me. And I just need you. We'll be able to help each other through anything at all, if we just say strong together."

I interlaced her fingers with mine. She smelled like the shampoo that she had just used to wash her hair, along with the minty body wash that I used to soap her up. I kissed her forehead and held her tight. "You're right, Dalilah. We're going to get through this. There's nothing that we can't do together. Just wait and see."

"I will, Luke. I have faith."

# Chapter Seventeen

## DALILAH

I slept well the previous evening. I was completely satisfied, sexually, by my romp with Luke in the shower. Serena's bed was totally comfortable, and the bedroom where we were staying was totally cute. She had excellent taste, really, with her choice of furniture, wall colors and drapes. Everything was color coordinated, without being too matchy-matchy. I felt comfortable being there.

So, I felt, all in all, that I was prepared as I ever could be to see my new lawyer. I had money for her retainer, courtesy of Luke, and it seemed that she was eager to see me and talk about my options.

There was only one problem, though – I knew that, once I saw her, and she filed what she had to file to get the ball rolling, there was no turning back. Nottingham would know about the baby. And I had no idea what to expect at that point.

Maybe he had moved on, and he would just let me have the divorce without incident?

Ha, fat chance on that.

Maybe he would go ballistic, knowing that I was having Luke's baby. He had proven, in the past, that he could be completely stalky. Would he resort to stalking me again? Would he come over here, and confront me, and maybe lose his temper with Luke and me? That seemed a more likely scenario.

Or, perhaps he would just quietly let his slimy lawyer speak for him. That wouldn't be the worst thing in the world, because I thought that Marissa could probably take him, knowing what I knew about Marissa and about Nottingham's lawyer.

Then it would just be up to the judge to decide. I hoped and prayed that we could get a sympathetic judge who would look at the evidence and decide that the best interest of the child would clearly not be with a man who was married to me for only like a month, even if he did have all kinds of money.

Then there would also be the idea that we might have to get down into the mud with this guy. I might have to bring out the beating that he gave me, the one that caused me to flee his house. Not to mention how he tried to frame Luke. And there might be any number of things that we would need to bring out in order to win this case. To show the judge that nobody's interest would be served by letting Nottingham anywhere near this baby in the future.

As much as I wanted this all to be a slam-dunk, I knew, in my heart, that it probably wouldn't be.

Luke wanted to go with me to see Marissa, but I encouraged him to go and see about his new co-op instead. I knew that the co-op was important to him, too, because it was his best chance to start making a good income and get some excellent contacts. With the boost that he already got through his premiere, he would have a good footing with those other artists, even if Nottingham had poisoned the well. He might not have the same chance to make it huge in the art world that he would have had Nottingham not pulled the rug out from under him, but he did have a chance to slowly make a name for himself with other unknowns.

To say that he was excited about this prospect underestimated the issue.

"Oh, Dalilah, come on," he had said, when I told him to go and see about the co-op. "I need to be there with you when you talk to your lawyer."

"I love you, Luke, but, really, I can handle this. Besides, if you go with me, there would be no confidentiality in anything that she and I say to one another. That might be a factor in the coming months. So, you would just have to wait out in the waiting room, and that's no fun for you."

So, Luke reluctantly went to the co-op instead of going with me.

And, as I sat on the bus that would take me to Marissa's office in Midtown, I wondered to myself why I didn't want Luke to come with me. Truth be told, despite the fact that I craved his protection, love and the sense of security he brought me, there was also just a little part of me that also craved independence still.

I was such a dichotomy, even to myself. Being in a relationship had changed me, for sure, because I definitely felt like a part of a unit. But this new me always fought with the old me. The old me, who really didn't need anybody, nor wanted to depend on anyone at all. The old me was buried, as much as I could bury her, but still, she came out at some inopportune times.

Like right then, going to Marissa's law office.

I GOT TO HER OFFICE, and went to see her. She summoned me almost as soon as I got there, and I followed her into her office and sat down across from her, feeling very nervous.

"Here," she said, giving me a glass of water. "You look like you might need this."

"I do," I said. "Well, okay, then. I'm going to file for divorce, and I'm going to admit on the divorce petition that I'm currently pregnant." I took a deep breath. "Why am I so terrified of this?"

"Well, don't be terrified just yet. Number one, we don't know what judge we're going to draw. Number two, I really don't know whom Nottingham is going to use for his attorney. I mean, he has always used Steve Singleton, but it's entirely possible that he'll use someone else who specializes in family law." She shook her head. "I'd rather have Steve Singleton, to tell you the truth. Steve might be an aggressive jerk, but I think that I could run circles around him as far as knowing the law in this area. But, if Nottingham gets somebody who specializes in family law, then all bets are off, even more than before."

I drew a breath. "I'm sorry. I was hoping that you might make me feel better about my prospects, not worse."

"Well, I just wanted you to be prepared, that's all. Now, let's get down to business." She turned to her computer and started typing. "You and Blake Nottingham were married on what day?"

I took a deep breath. "December 10 of last year."

She went on, asking me the basic questions for the petition. She asked when we were separated, how much property or assets were accumulated during the time that we were living under the same roof, when I conceived, and other questions that would help her compose the basic petition for divorce in New York State.

After about an hour of the housekeeping business that she needed to do to get the ball rolling, she printed out the petition for divorce and had me look it over. I approved it, and she signed it as my attorney and summoned her courier. She gave the courier the petition, along with my filing fee.

"So," she said, looking at my face after she gave the courier my petition to file at the courthouse. "What are you thinking?"

"To be honest? I'm trying very hard to stop myself from tackling that courier and snatching my petition away from him."

"That's a common feeling," she said. "Most of my clients are so happy to be doing this, yet absolutely dreading it at the same time."

"Well, that would certainly describe me," I said. "Especially the dreading part. I don't really know what to expect to happen when Nottingham gets that petition. I only know that it probably won't be good. Especially when he finds out about the baby."

"Well, you might actually find yourself relieved when Nottingham gets it. No matter his reaction. Because what's done is done."

"That's very true. At least the unknown will be known by then."

Marissa nodded. "If you don't mind my asking, why did you and Mr. Nottingham get married? I'm always curious about that when I get a client who wants to end a short-term marriage."

"I married him to help the man that I really love," I said. Then, seeing her confused expression, I went into the whole story of why Nottingham and I got together.

"I see," Marissa said, after I told her the sorry tale. "That's very noble of you, really, to do that. I'm very sorry that it came to this, though."

"I know," I said.

"Well," she said. "I need to know more about Nottingham and Luke. One of the factors in judging the best interest of the child in this situation, of course, is the relative merit of both of the potential fathers. What would you say that would be negative about Luke?"

I put my hand on my chin, thinking about that. "Not much, to be honest. He's really an awesome guy. Just a stand-up person. He has integrity, he's very even-tempered and patient, and he's very supportive and loving." I also could have told her that he's the sexiest man alive, but that wouldn't exactly be relevant here.

"Sounds good," she said. "I'm also going to have to know more about his financials. The judge is going to want to see if he has the finances to support a baby."

I briefly started to panic when she said that. Because Luke's financials, so far, were far from steady. I really hoped that he could blossom in his new co-op, assuming that these artists would allow him in, but it would be a hard slog. Unless, of course, Luke could parlay at least one of the wealthy benefactors who attended his premiere, and loved him, into a steady gig. But, since most of those wealthy benefactors were tight with Nottingham, that didn't seem likely.

"Well, right now, he has about $60,000 in the bank. He's an artist, of course, but he's also a song-writer. He just sold four of his songs to a group that just signed on to Gallagher Records, so the royalties from that could be substantial." I looked down at my hands, and tried to stop them from nervously fluttering.

Marissa nodded her head. "Well, that could be our Achilles Heel. It sounds like his future financial prospects are far from certain right now. I hope that I don't cause offense by saying this, but artists often aren't looked upon kindly by judges who are trying to ascertain the ability to support a child long-term."

I opened my mouth, about to protest that Luke was different, because he had enormous talent, then shut it again. I knew that she was right.

"So, what do you think we should do?" I asked.

"Drag out the proceedings as long as possible, which would give

Luke a chance to find his footing, career-wise. You say that he just started with his co-op, correct?"

"Yes," I said, weakly. "I hope to do the same. It's just been so difficult concentrating and trying to get motivated with all these messes hanging over my head. I'm sure you understand."

"Of course," she said. "The problem, of course, is that Nottingham has substantial resources. I hate to say it in such a crass way, but judges do look at that type of thing in considering a case like this."

"I figured that." I rolled my eyes. "I think that's crass, of course. That type of thing shouldn't matter as much as the fact that Luke and I will love this baby very much, and Nottingham, well, I don't see him in quite the same light."

"There are other things that the judge will take into account, of course. Such as the fact that you and Luke appear to be in a solid relationship, while Nottingham isn't, from what I can tell. And I can certainly bring up the issue of Nottingham beating you. That would weigh in your favor as well."

I twiddled my thumbs and took a deep breath. "I've been thinking about that. And I'm still too scared to use that. I don't know what Nottingham is capable of. If I make that public, then he might do something really rash."

"It's up to you, of course. But, as your counselor, I would strongly suggest that the beating become a part of you defense. It could very well be something that could change the course of proceedings."

There was a lot, really, that I could bring into the custody case, if I wanted to get down and dirty. Nottingham's sexual proclivities, for instance, and I was quite sure that there was much more to be known about him. But I still wasn't entirely sure that I was going to be up for such a fight.

Which was why, really, I ran in the first place. I didn't have the energy for a fight. I was still scared of that man, and I still couldn't quite fathom the depths of what he was capable of to get exactly what he wanted from me.

And I still had no desire to find out.

# Chapter Eighteen

I made my way to the artist's co-op, which was just a few blocks away from Serena's home, conveniently enough. I still felt badly about not going with Dalilah to her appointment with her attorney, but she insisted that she didn't want me there. For whatever reason. I was a tad bit hurt, but, at the same time, I knew that she was probably right. I probably should go and meet the other artists in this group, to make sure that they want me as a part of their cooperative and to also see what they were like.

I got to the building, which was a renovated commercial building that had been turned into studio lofts ranging in square footage from 1,500 to around 5,000 square feet. There was one artist, in particular, that I was supposed to make contact with. Her name was J.J. Mullens, and her medium was sculpting. So, when I got to the building, I immediately found her studio and went to introduce myself.

"Hello," I said to the petite and attractive woman. "My name is Luke Roberts. I was referred here by Marcella Taylor. She told me that she had talked to you about joining your cooperative."

She shook my hand. "It's very good to meet you. I remember you, too. I remember the show that you had back in December. You drew quite a crowd, and a lot of attention. I really love your aesthetic, too."

"Well, thanks," I said, looking around her enormous studio at some of the pieces she was working on. "I think that the feeling is mutual."

"Let me tell you about our cooperative," she said. "Basically, we're 20 artists who are pooling resources. We all got together to rent spaces in this building, and we have also invested in a gallery down the street from here – the Thiessen Gallery, which is named after one of our prominent members who took his life last year. We require a buy-in of $20,000, to offset the costs of buying the gallery, as well as monthly dues, assuming that you want to rent a space in this building."

I swallowed, hard. I wondered to myself just how long Serena was going to allow Dalilah and me to live with her, and if she soon was going to require us to pay some type of rent.

"How much are the monthly dues?" I asked.

"It depends on how large of space you want. We charge by the square footage. Basically, we start at $1500 for the smallest studio and go up from there. Included in your dues, though, is all the advantages of being a part of this co-op. Our group organizes fund-raisers on a monthly basis, and we really talk each other up on social media. The gallery has events almost every week, and they've become more and more popular each week. They're usually cocktail parties and wine-tasting, but we've also hosted retrospectives of prominent artists and poetry readings. We also try to find opportunities for tie-ins with large New York events. We're constantly looking for new, fresh ways to get the word out about our artists."

"Sounds like there are lots of opportunities here for exposure. I really like the idea of cross-promotion." Still, even as I talked to her, I felt a well of nervous energy bubbling up. Paying this cooperative $20,000 up front, plus $1500 a month, on top of paying Dalilah's legal bills....unless I got hustling soon, I was going to be broke within a matter of months. Perhaps I would be broke even sooner than that.

JJ continued. "Well, there are lots of good opportunities here. And, I'll confess, when Marcella told me about you, I got excited. You do have the ability to generate a lot of enthusiasm for your work. I was wondering, though, what happened with your premiere. It seemed that you were going to take off, but then I never heard more about it."

"Well, that's difficult to explain," I said. "It has something to do with the gallery owner being obsessed with my girlfriend, and apparently getting me blackballed with the elite benefactors who can make or break an artist in this town. So, now, I'm starting from square one, just like you guys."

"Oh, that's a shame," she said. "Tough break, huh? Well, at any rate, if you're interested in getting a leg up, you should consider joining us. We have the perfect studio for you, and everybody in this group is cool and chill. And I know that your girlfriend is also an artist, and a substantial one at that. She could join us, too, for the same fee."

"Well, that might be difficult to swing," I said.

JJ looked at me questioningly. "Her parents are super-rich, aren't they?"

"Yeah," I said. "But she won't allow them to support her. She's very proud like that."

Of course, Dalilah didn't mind staying with people while we figured everything out. I never asked her about this apparent discrepancy in how she thought about being supported, and wondered if she thought about that one herself.

"Well, maybe if she broaches it in terms of an investment for her parents or a loan or something like that. You should talk to her about that."

"I certainly will."


I WENT BACK TO SERENA'S AND WAITED FOR DALILAH TO RETURN. The information at the cooperative was certainly good to have, but I needed to talk to Dalilah before I made this commitment. I was sure that she would be supportive, but we had to look at our finances to make everything work out.

She got back around 5 that evening, looking tired and blue. I went over to her, and put my arm around her, and led her onto the couch.

"I did it," she said. "And the wrath of the Nottingham will soon be upon us, I predict. I've spent this past three hours just wondering around the city in a daze. I'm so apprehensive about this, you just have no idea." She looked around. "Where's Serena?"

"She left a note. She's out visiting a sick friend, and will be back later on tonight." I stroked her cheek and kissed her forehead. "I wish that there was something that I could say to you that will help you. I know how stressed you are, though, and I admit that I worry about you and about Olivia."

"I know, Luke. This stress isn't good for me. I have a pre-natal checkup tomorrow, the first one with this particular doctor, and I'm quite sure that things are going to be okay. But I do think about the fact that the doctor in London told me that I might have a difficult pregnancy because of my hormone levels not being in check. I'm trying to do everything right, Luke, but it's hard. It's hard because of the stress."

We talked a bit more about the lawyer, and I told her about the co-op.

"That sounds great, Luke," she said. "I think that you can really take advantage of that. Cross-promotion with other artists is always a good thing. Also good is the fact that it sounds that they actively promote their gallery. I've read stuff about the Thiessen Gallery, and it sounds like it's up and coming. I say go for it."

So, it was decided. I would buy into the cooperative and try to get one of the smaller spaces until things started to roll.

Dalilah was quiet for a few minutes. "Well, I don't want to put further pressure on you, but I feel that I have to. Your finances are going to come into play in the custody issue. I'm sure that probably isn't news to you."

I nodded. That wasn't news to me at all. I expected that, in fact. "I know. That means that I probably need to get going, doesn't it? I mean, the judge might rule against terminating Nottingham's rights just because there's such a disparity in resources between him and me. As much as that sucks."

"Well, yes, but, as you know, there are lots of other factors that come into play. She wants me to go balls to the wall and bring in Nottingham's visits to the sex clubs and his beating of me, and she's looking into his background to find out any other dirt that might come up. I'm nervous about all that, though. I don't know, Luke, I just have a bad feeling about doing all of that. I'm not at all sure that I want to really unleash the beast, so to speak. He might really find a way to get down and dirty if I do."

"So, what are you going to do?"

"Wait and see what happens when he is served. See what kind of an opening volley his lawyer makes. See who is lawyer is even going to be – it might be Steve Singleton, and it might be somebody else who's more experienced in the field of family law. So many factors are going to come into play here. I'm guessing that what happens with Nottingham's lawyer is going to dictate how Marissa and I decide to approach this. We're going to get ready for anything, though."

"I guess it's pointless to speculate, though, huh?" I asked her. "Well, let's not get too into the weeds just yet. If it's possible, let's take things one day at a time."

She took a deep breath. "Hmmm, well, I certainly could use some TLC. Let's go into the bedroom to see if we can drum some up."

I smiled. "Let's go for it," I said.

We went upstairs, and immediately took off our clothes and went for it.

# *Chapter Nineteen*

## DALILAH

Exactly one week after I filed my divorce petition with Marissa, the shit hit the proverbial fan. Nottingham made his first reappearance since I the night of my beating, and, to my dismay, he showed up right at Serena's door.

"I can't talk to you," I told him through the door, after I looked in the peephole and saw him standing on Serena's front porch. "We're in active litigation here, so you're lawyer is going to have to talk to my lawyer. That's how it works."

"That isn't how it's going to work here, Dalilah," he said calmly from the other side of the door. "You and I need to talk about this, face to face, adult to adult. You have to talk to me, if you want this to at all go the way that you're envisioning."

I looked at Serena, who was listening to every word between Nottingham and me. Luke, for his part, was down at his new studio, creating and trying to make friends with the other artists down there. Serena raised an eyebrow. "You better let him in," she said. "I have a strong feeling that, if you don't, there's going to be hell to pay."

"There's going to be hell to pay either way," I said. Then I reluctantly opened the door. I faced Nottingham and said "how did you find me?"

"Dalilah," Nottingham said. "If you don't know by now that I have ways of tracking you down, anywhere you think that you're safe hiding, then you really have very little common sense. I know that you're extremely intelligent, of course, but you obviously have some blind spots that I have enjoyed manipulating."

I took a deep breath. "Okay, then, you found me." I waited to say anything more."

"Yes," he said. "And, if you didn't come back to the States from London, I would have tracked you down there, too." He shook his head. "Really, Dalilah. Why you ever thought that I wouldn't be able to find you, I don't know. How was it staying with Liam Gallagher?"

I put my chin up, determined not to show the panic I was feeling as he spoke. "It was great, thanks for asking. Liam's place is gorgeous and peaceful. It really gave me a chance to try to think things through."

"Well," he said, "are you going to invite me in?"

"No," I said. "We can talk right here."

He shook his head. "Dalilah. I would think that, with the information I have about some friends of yours, not to mention your father, you would be a bit more hospitable to me."

"My father?" I said, feeling my heart drop to my shoes. "What does he have to do with any of this?"

"Do I need to spell it out?" he asked. "In front of your hostess here? If not, I suggest that you and I go somewhere and talk. We need to negotiate the custody issues with my child."

"It's not your child," I said.

"Legally it is. And, once you hear what I have to say, I think that you're probably going to end up not wanting to fight me. That's my prediction, anyhow."

I started breathing faster. *What did he know, and how did he know it?* "No way. You won't get your hands on this child. Ever. This child belongs to Luke, not to you. I'll fight you to the death for this. I will."

Nottingham shook his head. "Well, then, perhaps the entire world needs to know exactly what type of guy your father is. He seems so charitable and philanthropic. And Nick, well, he's the senior managing partner of one of the richest architectural firms in the world. He has a reputation, that's for sure, and it's a good one. But it might not be for long."

I heard the cryptic words, and my heart fell further. It was like an elevator that was snapped from its cables, plummeting down 100 stories with breakneck speed. "I don't know what you're talking about," I said.

Nottingham just screwed up his face. "Yes, you do. Now, meet me at the restaurant down the street, and you and I will talk about this. I'll see you in about fifteen minutes."

I shut the door, and tried to catch my breath. I felt a little fluttering in my abdomen, and wondered if this was one of the first movements that I felt from my little one. "It's going to be okay, Olivia, it's going to be just fine. It's going to be fine." I turned to Serena, who was standing right behind me. "I have to meet him down at that restaurant on the end of the block." I tried hard not to burst into tears.

Serena held me in her arms. "Go down and meet him," she said. "Sounds serious."

I looked at her. I wanted her to tell me that it was all going to turn out okay. I knew that sometimes Serena had foresight on such things, and if she said that it would all turn out, then it would. I really and truly believed that to be true.

"Serena, what do you feel about this? It doesn't sound so good. If Nottingham has the kind of information that I'm afraid that he does...it won't be good at all. Please, do you have any kind of feeling or hunch about this?"

Serena just shook her head. "Oh, I wish that I could turn it off and on like that, but I can't. It pretty much comes in flashes, when I'm least expecting it. So, no, I don't have any kind of foresight on what is going to happen here. I would tell you if I did, though. I promise."

I nodded my head. "I understand. Well, I guess I better go down there."

At that, I went out the door to meet my certain doom.

I GOT TO THE RESTAURANT, AND NOTTINGHAM WAS WAITING FOR ME. I sat down across from him, and folded my hands in front of me. He raised his eyebrow, and ordered a martini for himself. He turned to me. "I assume that you want something non-alcoholic. At least you better. I certainly don't want my child to have any kind of problems due to your bad habits. That goes for your marijuana use, too. I would hope that would go without saying, but, with you, I just never know." Then he shook his head.

"Yes," I said, as calmly as possible. "Please order me a Club Soda with a twist of lime."

He did so, and ordered lunch for both of us. Just like old times – he never bothered to ask me what I wanted. He just ordered.

"Okay," I said. "I'm here. You need to talk to me."

"Yes," he said. "I want you to drop your contesting of my rights to my child. I understand that I probably won't have full custody, nor do I want that. I do have a business to run, although I'm currently involved in a new, stable relationship with a very nurturing woman. She told me that she would be more than happy to help me raise this child."

"This isn't your child," I said. "The DNA test proves that." At that, I took the results of the DNA test out of my purse. It was a copy of what I got from the laboratory in England.

Nottingham took the paper from my hands, and then lit it on fire with the candle on the table. "That's what I think about these test results. They're not worth a dime in court, you know. Not when the child was conceived while you were married to me."

"I realize that," I said. "But I might get a judge who will accept these test results and declare Luke the father. Which would mean that your rights would be terminated."

"I wouldn't count on that," he said. "I'm very friendly with most of the bench, and, besides, I have an ace in the hole."

I held my breath, waiting for the other shoe to drop. "Oh?" I asked, as calmly as I could. "And what ace would that be?"

"I think you know."

"Know what?"

"Dalilah," he said. "I did something to you awhile ago that I'm quite sure that you're not aware of. It wasn't legal, but, that doesn't matter at this point. When you were going to marry me, I put a recording device on your phone. I basically wanted to make sure that you weren't seeing Luke on the sly. I was impressed, by the way, by your stellar performance in dumping him. I probably couldn't have done a better job myself."

*A recording device. How did I not suspect?* "Okay," I said. "So, you found out that I had dumped Luke, just like you asked, and I never saw him behind your back."

Nottingham smiled. "You're not a stupid person, by any stretch of the imagination. And your mind is a devious one, but not as much as mine. I can always stay one step ahead of you, Dalilah. Because I'm willing to do whatever it takes to make sure that you pay for fucking me over the way that you have."

I tried to control my temper. "Fucking you over? You beat me. I probably would have stayed with you if you wouldn't have done that. Even though I despised you, and I still do. I would have stayed with you, because I wanted Luke to have his shot that much. So, my leaving you had everything to do with your actions. Don't tell me that I fucked you over, you bastard."

I braced myself for what was coming next. "You fucked me over by going to him the night of his premiere, instead of coming right home to me. But, that's neither here nor there, is it?" He smiled, evidently delighted at my no-doubt stricken expression. "Now, Dalilah, I'm quite sure that you know what all of this is leading up to, don't you?"

I tried to shake my head, but I knew that I did it weakly.

"Oh, come on," he said. "Again, you aren't stupid. Now, I know about what your father's best friend Nick did all those years ago. I know it because you ran your mouth to Nick just before you and I were married. That has always been my ace in the hole."

Crash! The elevator just ran aground, killing everyone on board. Not that this was a surprise. I knew it was coming, from his first cryptic words to me on Serena's porch.

*Don't cry Dalilah, don't cry. And don't commit to anything right now. Buy some time. Buy some time.*

I took an enormous breath, and tried to think of something. But what came out of my mouth was probably something that was going to get me into deeper trouble. As if I could possibly get into deeper trouble than I already was at this point.

"Oh, yeah? Well, let's just say that I have some dirt on you, too. We'll see who blinks first." I was bluffing. I didn't have any dirt on him, at all, but I was pretty certain that he was dirty in some way. I hoped that my words activated some kind of panic in him, and that he really thought that I did have something on him.

He looked unruffled. "Oh, really, Dalilah? You do." Then he chuckled and took another sip of his drink. "You're bluffing. I know it. What dirt do you have on me, pray tell?"

I was encouraged by his reaction. He tried to hide it, but I saw just a flicker of fear in his eyes. *He does have something to hide. I just need to find out what it is.*

"I'll never tell. Let's just say that, if you try to get my father and Nick in trouble, you're gonna see exactly what kind of dirt I have on you. And you'll be in prison. Now, what you know about Nick – the statute of limitations has run on those crimes."

"The statute never runs on murder," he said. "But go on."

"It wasn't a murder. That man committed suicide. All the other crimes that were committed – the statute has long since passed."

"Really Dalilah? If you get some eager beaver prosecutor on the case, you really think that he or she won't be able to make the case that what happened was a murder? I agree, it's a grey area, but I think that you know it could go either way. I can't believe that you want to take that chance. Take the chance that your beloved friend will spend the rest of their lives behind bars. And your father too – after all, the crime was recorded on his computer, so chances are good that he had something to do with it."

I inwardly cursed myself. Cursed myself for bringing the subject up to Nick. Cursed myself for being so goddamned nosy that I was a hacker, just for shits and grins, which made me come across that video. Cursed myself for not realizing that Nottingham was underhanded enough to do something like bug me.

How could I have been so naïve?

*Gut check time.* But I was gambling with my father's future, not to mention Nick's. I was blindsided by this revelation, but I had to think on my feet.

I raised my chin. "Oh, well, what you did was just as illegal," I said. "You take me down, and I'll take you down. You take my father down, and you're going down with him. Maybe you guys can wave hello to one another in the penitentiary yard."

Again, the flicker of fear ran through his eyes for just a millisecond. If it wasn't for that tiny little involuntary flicker, I probably would have backed down and agreed to anything that he wanted. But I saw that flicker, and I knew that I was onto something.

It was going to be a matter of finding out exactly what it was that I was onto. But there was something there.

Then he smiled. "You don't have anything on me, Dalilah. But, I'll bite. Lay your cards out on the table."

"No way," I said. "I got you good, but there's no way that I'm going to give you a chance to cover up your tracks." I raised my eyebrow, wondering if there was more than one illegal thing he was up to behind the scenes. If there was, then he was probably wondering, in his mind, exactly what goody I was going to spring.

He screwed up his face. "You don't have anything. Now, let's see. How about I see the prosecutor today to start looking into the death of Paul Lucas? Maybe it's time to reopen a cold case, huh?"

I took a deep breath. "I don't think so. No prosecutor is going to reopen that case. You have no proof of anything. Unless, of course, you want to use the recording that you made of me. But you and I both know that would never give anybody probable cause of anything, because what you did in recording me was clearly illegal. On the other hand, I got some pretty good proof of all the dirty business that you're up to."

The look in his eyes said *you little bitch.* "Hm. Well, you think that you're the only one who knows how to hack? Let's just say that I have somebody who has that same capability, and I got video proof of what he did."

I put on my poker face and examined him. I didn't believe him about that. Something told me that he was now the one who was bluffing. If he did have that video, then all of us would be in this shit hole. If he didn't, then he probably would have a very tough time trying to get the case re-opened. Using an illegal recording of me spouting off my mouth wouldn't be enough to re-open that case, that was for sure.

My mind whirled. I had a tough time finding the video, and I had gotten pretty good at hacking. At the point when I found it, I probably could have hacked the Department of Defense. Not that there weren't people in the world who were even better than that, and god knew that Nottingham had the resources to hire someone who could do that.

Nottingham smiled. "You know, it's all pretty ironic. You're so brilliant that you were able to hack Nick's computer and find something that he had erased off his hard drive a long time before that. Yet you had no idea that I bugged your phone. Like I said, you clearly have a blind spot in your intelligence. But maybe it was just a case of clear naiveté."

At that point, I wanted to lunge at him. Put my hands around his neck and strangle him.

Who was going to blink first?

"Okay," I finally said. "You go to the prosecutor, and you see what will happen. As I said, if you take us down, you're going down right along with us. One thing is for sure, though. You will never, and I mean never, get custody of this child. In any way, shape or form."

At that, I got up from the table and walked out the door.

# Chapter Twenty

As I walked away from Nottingham in the restaurant, I pulled my coat around me and tried to fight off the biting wind. March was certainly coming in like a lion, just as it was supposed to.

I alighted at Serena's, and sat down in her chair.

"Dalilah," she said. "Let me fix you a cup of tea. You look like you need it."

"Actually, I need a drink," I said. "A real drink. And, if I weren't pregnant, that would be exactly what I would have right now."

"That bad, huh?"

"You don't know the half of it." I fought the feeling that I was going to absolutely break down. "I need to make a phone call really quick. I don't know if I can do it, though. I'm too out of sorts right now."

"Let me call Luke," Serena said. "And he'll make any phone calls you need. I would make the calls, if you like, but I probably don't know these people, so maybe it wouldn't be such a great idea."

"Yes, please, call him," I said. "I need him. And I need him to call some people for me." I also needed to talk to him. He might as well know what I caused in this regard by trying to bring this up to Nick after all these years. If it weren't for me and my big mouth, Nottingham wouldn't have any kind of ammunition to use against me. I hated myself for giving him that.

At that, Serena called Luke. "He'll be here in ten minutes," she said. Then she went to join me on the couch. "So, tell me what's going on?"

I shook my head. "I can't right now. I just can't talk about it. I'm so sorry. I'm just kind of stunned, really. And ashamed of myself. Luke is probably going to hate me when he hears the latest on what's going on.

"It can't be as bad as all that," she said. "Could it?"

"Oh, yes. Yes, it can. But I need to have a meeting with my parents and my Uncle Nick, because they're going to be directly implicated on what is happening." I nervously thought about my meeting with Nottingham. Was he going to bring us all under?

LUKE APPEARED AT SERENA'S WITHIN TEN MINUTES. He saw my face, which must have been white as a sheet, and immediately rushed to my side. "What is it?" he asked. "There's not something wrong with Olivia, is there?" He put his hand in my hair, and kissed my cheek lightly.

When I saw him, I couldn't help it. I burst into tears. I had been wanting to cry ever since I had my little meeting with Nottingham, but I had to force it down while I faced him. But I felt that I had permission, finally, to break down, so that was exactly what I did.

Luke looked at Serena desperately. "What's going on? Is Dalilah okay physically? Is the baby okay? She's not bleeding again, is she?"

"The baby seems to be fine," Serena said, while I cried hysterically. "At least, Dalilah said nothing about the baby when she arrived here."

"What did she say?"

"She said that she had to make some phone calls, but that she wasn't up to it. I think that she wants you to make the phone calls."

I just nodded my head. "Call my dad," I choked out. "And have him call Nick. Have them meet me here as soon as they can. Please."

"Okay," he said. At that, he called my father. "Ryan," he said. "This is Luke....Dalilah asked me to call you....I'm doing okay, how are you?....yes, yes....well, we're back in the States, I'm surprised Dalilah hasn't told you....she wants to meet you here at my sister Serena's.....as soon as you can....and she wants you to call Nick, too, and have him meet us here, too....Serena's address is------.......today, if possible....I have no idea why she wants to talk to you....see you then....you take care too."

Luke got off the phone. "Okay, they'll be here this evening. We can go out to dinner, if you like."

"I'll make dinner," Serena offered.

I was feeling calmer, in that I stopped crying. But I still was at a loss for words.

"Dalilah's parents are vegans," Luke said. "Is that okay?"

"Luke," Serena said. "I'm also a vegan. I guess you aren't overly observant, but that's okay."

Luke's face turned red. "Come to think of it, you really didn't eat that turkey at Christmas. I guess I didn't really think about it."

Serena put her arm around Luke. "Kid, there's a lot you don't know about me. But that's my fault entirely." She winked at both of us. "I'm a mean vegan cook, too. Trust me, you won't miss the animal products."

"Well, okay, then," Luke said. "Thanks, Serena, in advance. Can I go to the store or anything for whatever you need?"

Serena shook her head. "I'll make some eggplant parmesan, without the parmesan, of course – just breaded eggplant, fried in walnut oil, topped with marinara. Serve it was some linguini and bread with olive oil, and my special recipe vegan brownies, and it's a really great meal. And salad, too. I like to throw all kinds of stuff in my salads – nuts, fruits, avocados, croutons."

"Sounds awesome," Luke said. "Well, okay, then, I guess it's settled. We'll have dinner here."

Then he turned to me. "Okay, Dalilah, you need to talk to me. I don't particularly want to be blindsided when I see what you're going to say to your parents and Nick."

*Oh, god.* Well, I was going to have to come clean with Luke. I had no idea how he was going to react.

I shook my head. "Well, let's see. Where do I begin?"

"Wherever you want to begin," he said.

"Okay. Well. I'll just start with how I was when I was in 12. I was a frustrated pre-teen. Bored with school, bored with life. I didn't feel that

I had an artistic voice anymore, so I was just a bit numb. I needed a challenge in my life, or else I was just going to scream."

"Go on," Luke said. He looked confused, but, for his part, he seemed to be okay.

"Hold on," I said. I went to the other room, and took out my purse. I had no idea how much of a range that little recording device had.

I went out to the living room, and handed the phone to Serena. "Could you do me a favor? Could you take this phone down to Luke's new studio? I'll explain later."

She nodded. "I'll be back in about ten minutes or so."

"Thanks," I said.

Luke looked more confused than ever.

"I'm so sorry, Luke," I said. "This will all come together, I promise. But I really want Serena to know everything, too, because she might be able to help out. So, I need to wait until she gets back to tell you the rest of the sorry story."

Serena was back within 10 minutes, and she sat down.

"Okay," I said. "I was just talking about how bored I was when I was young, and how I wanted a challenge. Well, I decided to teach myself to hack computers. It was just a puzzle for me, a game. I got all nosy, looked at my dad's computers and my mom's. Why, I don't really know. That's just how I was. I was not only bored, but I was nosy, too." I shook my head. "I shouldn't have done that. It wasn't right."

Luke said nothing, just held my hand, and continued to look concerned.

"Anyhow, well, I found something. I was really into it, and I went through his files that he had erased off his hard drive. I was just so thrilled that I could find old files like that. I was giddy. Stupid me. But, you know, when you get that good at hacking, it was a high. You know, I could find things that he was desperate to hide. Things that he took a lot of time and effort to erase. And, well, I found something. Something very serious."

Serena and Luke both were looking concerned.

I took a deep breath. I had to trust Serena and Luke not to take this information that I was going to tell them, and not use it against me, or, god forbid, Nick and my dad, in the future. I trusted Luke, implicitly.

And something told me that I could also trust Serena. I hoped that my gut wasn't wrong about that. It could be not such a good thing.

Still, I decided that I couldn't use my gut, there. Not when it was Nick and my father's future at stake. "Serena, god, I'm so sorry. But I can't tell you this. It isn't my story to tell, really. It's Nick's and my dad's."

She looked stricken, and I felt bad. Perhaps I could tell her that Nottingham was blackmailing me, and see if she could help out, without telling her exactly what information Nottingham was using against me.

"I understand," she said. "I'll be out on the deck, and, when you want me to come in, I'll be back."

"Thanks," I said. "I'm so sorry, if it was my story, only, I'd tell you. But I can't, because there are so many others implicated in this."

She nodded, and, at that, she went to her back balcony and sat down. I felt awful. I just kicked her out of her own home.

"Go on, Dalilah," Luke said.

"I'm trusting you with this, Luke. The fact that I'm willing to tell you all of this shows just how much I trust you."

"Sounds really serious," he said. "But go on."

"Well," I said. "I found a video of Nick. He was threatening this guy, Paul Lucas. He was telling this guy that he had to commit suicide, because if this guy didn't commit suicide, he, Nick, would turn him in for things that he did. Apparently this Paul was a serial rapist, and he had admitted that he was raping young girls for years. Hundreds of them. This guy had raped my Aunt Scotty, too, for years. So, he was a bad, bad man, to say the least."

Luke's face was turning white. "Egads," he said. "Talk about heavy." He shook his head. "What an awful scenario." He visibly shuddered. "If anybody raped you, I think that I would be tempted to do the same. Any man would. But, I don't think that I would have the guts to go through with it."

I took a deep breath. "Well, Nick, you have to understand him. He's no shrinking violet, by any means. He's an awesome guy, but he definitely has the guts to make the heavy choices. Not to mention morally ambiguous ones."

"Okay," Luke said. "Well, go on. I'm listening."

"Well," I said. "This video ended with this Paul guy putting a gun in his mouth and pulling the trigger."

I tried to gauge Luke's reaction, but I couldn't. He looked like he was proud of Nick for doing it, yet, at the same time, horrified that Nick would do something like that.

Kind of like the way that I felt when I found the video.

"I think that I know where this is going," Luke said. "But, go on."

"You're going to hate me," I said. "But I have to get it out in the open. When I was going to marry Nottingham, I knew that my dad was going to freak out. I wanted Nick on my side. Nick is my father's most trusted friend. They've gone through everything together. So, I wanted Nick to talk to my dad. Tell him that Nottingham wasn't a bad guy. After all, Nick has apparently known Nottingham for awhile. That was how I first encountered Nottingham, was at one of Nick's parties."

Now, Luke's face was starting to change. He shook his head. "You didn't. Please tell me you didn't."

*Time to rip off the Band-Aid, and let the chips fall where they may.* "I did. Nick wasn't playing along, so I casually told him that I knew what he did. For a brief moment, I thought that I would use it against him, or at least make him think that I was going to use it against him. But I backed off of that immediately. Almost as soon as I said it, I back-tracked, and told him that I would never hold that over his head. I felt bad about bringing that up, immediately."

Luke was shaking his head. He looked like he was about to blow a gasket. He was also no longer holding my hand. Rather, he was running his hands through his thick hair. Then he got up, and started to pace.

I felt just a little panicky, but I forged on.

"Goddamn it," he finally said. "Goddamn it. I love you. You're the smartest woman I know. But how could you be so fucking stupid? I....I don't even know what to say. Why would go there? You find something out like that about someone you love, and this person that you love hasn't done anything to you. Yet, you're going to try to use that against him? Good lord, Dalilah, what the hell were you thinking?"

I fought back tears. "I was desperate, Luke. I wanted my dad to be on board with this Nottingham nonsense, and I thought that Nick would help with that. It was stupid, Luke, and there's no excuse for it."

"I see. I see." Luke continued to pace. "We're back to this, aren't we? We're back to things biting you on your ass, as they're going to do when you do things that are morally reprehensible. Goddamn it, why can't you see that? Hasn't anyone ever told you that if you're in a hole to stop digging?"

"I know, Luke. But I've made the decision not to do things underhanded. Remember? I made that decision when I had my dream about our daughter."

Luke was nodding his head, obviously not hearing my protestations about how I had changed. "And Nottingham knows about this, doesn't he? I bet he did something like bug your phone, and he knows it all."

"How did you know that was what happened?"

"Because he's as duplicitous as you are, Dalilah. Probably moreso. Which is why it's so ridiculous that you would ever have gotten involved with him at all. If you couldn't see that he's going to out-maneuver you at every turn, just because his mind is more devious than yours, then I don't know what to tell you."

I shook my head. "He told me that I have a blind spot in my intelligence, which is why he has been able to out- maneuver me, as you say. Always stay one step ahead. I guess he's right."

"You damned right, he's right. You obviously have a blind spot as big as Jupiter."

"So, now, Nottingham is threatening me. He said that if I don't give him custody of this baby, joint custody, he's going to bring down Nick and my dad."

Luke cocked his head. "Your dad. He's involved with this, too?"

I shrugged my shoulder. "I don't really know. I mean, the video was on my dad's computer, so I don't know what that means. I guess I need to find out more."

"Oh, god. Well, okay, so Nottingham knows. The first thing you do is clean up that phone. I have no idea how you're going to do that, because those devices are microscopic. I have no idea how you're going to find it. But, one thing's for sure, you can't get rid of that phone, because you don't want it falling into the wrong hands."

"That goes without saying," I said. "And, well, I told him that I had dirt on him, and that if he decided to play hard ball, that I would bring him down. When I said that, I think that I was onto something. I saw a bit of fear in his eyes when I said it. A flicker of fear. I was bluffing, of course, but I saw something in his eyes that makes me think that I really could bring him down if it came to that."

Luke shook his head. "Okay. Looks like we're going to have to fight fire with fire. I don't approve of this, of course. But we have to find something on him." He shook his head again. "Nothing else can really be done. We're completely backed into a corner, Dalilah, because of you. I hope you're happy."

I tried not to panic at Luke's words. He was clearly angry, and I hoped that he didn't really mean what he was saying.

I breathed in and out, in and out. I had to calm down. I was feeling panicky about the situation, and Luke's words made it all that much worse. Not that I blamed him for saying these things. I knew that he was frustrated. I didn't blame him. But I needed him to be on my side. No matter what I did, no matter how morally wrong I was, I needed him to tell me that he could understand why I would do these things. I needed him to forgive me, and understand how badly I wanted to change.

I felt a sense of keen relief, when he came over to me, and took my hand. "Dalilah," he said calmly. "I'm frustrated at the situation. I'm not going to tell you that you weren't wrong in what you did, because you clearly were. But what's done is done. We have go to forward. We have to go forward, and hopefully your dad and Nick can help with this."

I smiled. Luke wasn't going to leave me over this. He wasn't happy, but it seemed that he would continue to be on my side, and that meant the absolute world to me.

# Chapter Twenty-One

My mom, dad, Nick and Scotty arrived at Serena's home at 6 PM. I helped Serena prepare the food, and Luke went out and got some good scotch for Nick and my dad, along with some good wine for Scotty and my mom. I actually enjoyed helping Serena cook. It was relaxing, really, and I desperately needed to relax.

"So," Serena said to me. "I guess I need to make myself scarce, huh, after dinner? I mean, since you don't want me to know what's going on."

"I'm so sorry. This is your home. I wish that I could tell you, but it's just too risky."

She nodded. "Well, at any rate, I'll have the chance to meet your family, which is a good thing. I'm happy about that."

"Thanks so much for understanding," I said.

"That's okay," she said. "I've already made plans to see a friend of mine and catch up with her. It's not a problem."

MY MOM, DAD, NICK AND SCOTTY arrived at 6. They came in, and had a seat, and Luke got all of them a drink.

"Thanks, Luke," my dad said, "from the tone of your call today, I think that we're all going to need this."

"Well," Luke said. "You probably will. At any rate, we have some awesome food to eat. We have a lot to talk about, but after we eat."

Serena smiled. "We're like Italians. Everything is going to go down better after a good meal."

The dinner couldn't have gone better. Everything was delicious, and my dad and everybody tried to valiantly make small talk and get to know Serena. But, through it all, there was severe tension in the air. It could be cut like a knife.

After the vegan brownie dessert, and some after-dinner drinks, Serena excused herself. "Well, it's been awesome to meet all of you, but I have a friend to meet tonight."

Everybody stood up and gave her a hug. "It's been great meeting you, Serena," my dad said. "Thanks so much for being such a great hostess and welcoming us into your home. It really means a lot to us."

Everyone else said similar things to Serena, and she left with a smile.

After she left, my dad led off the charge. "Okay, now, Dalilah, let's not beat around the bush, here. You called us here, and you obviously have something on your mind. And, judging by your recent meetings that you have called with us, I would have to say that what's going on is probably something that's not so great. To say the least."

"Yes," I said. And then I launched into everything about how Nottingham was blackmailing me. I didn't have to tell them about the rest – about my hacking and all that, because, of course, they already knew that story.

My dad was shaking his head. "Okay. Well, then, we have a situation on our hands, don't we? To say the least."

"Of course," I said. "Listen, dad, I'm not all that clear, though. You were in on the Paul Lucas thing. Of that, I'm relatively certain. But what did you do? Were you just aware that he was doing it, or were you actively involved in planning it?"

My dad was quiet. "I was involved in planning it. Nick and I planned it together. I got my security firm involved in it. It was my computer that we used to record it. The entire plan was put together by Nick and me, side by side. So, if Nick is going down for this, I am too."

*Oh, god, I didn't know that my dad's neck was this much on the line.*
"I see," I said, and then looked around the room. My mom's face showed no surprise, so I guess she knew. Scotty's face showed no surprise, either.

They all knew about it. Of course. The four of them were tight, and they all formed a very strong circle of trust. They knew that nobody in that group would ever breathe a word about it.

I felt bad. If it weren't for me, that whole thing would remain buried. But, it kept coming up. It kept coming up, because of me. It should have remained buried with the bones of Paul Lucas.

I felt so guilty.

My dad shook his head. "What's done is done. Okay, then, it's time to bring out the big guns. We have no choice. You said that you thought that Nottingham was up to no good. From what you told me about him, and what Nick knows about him, I would think that you're probably correct about that."

"Where to begin, though, dad? How do we prove it?"

"I'll get my security firm on it," my dad said. "And hire a private investigator. There's going to be some shake-downs coming, I can sense it. I know some people who can get things done. They get things done within the bounds of what's legal, but they also can do things which aren't. They were involved in this Paul Lucas mess in the first place. They can out-Nottingham Nottingham, if that makes any sense at all."

I smiled. "Dad, thank-"

"No, Dalilah. I almost hate to get my security firm on it, because a part of me wants you to learn your lesson the hard way. But now that you've gotten all of us involved with your mess, it's time to come off the sidelines. We're going to come off the sidelines to clean up your mess, and cover up ours."

"Dalilah," Nick asked. "You know how I feel about what you did, hacking and threatening me. No need to revisit that. We do need to find out, though, if you have any suspicions at all that Nottingham was up to no good."

"Well, yes," I said, and I told them about the German conversation that I overheard. "I was going to try to hack him myself and find out about that trade, but I decided not to. But there is that. That's the only thing, though, that I heard that would make me think that he's doing something illegal."

"That's a good place to start," Nick said. "Have somebody look at all the trades that he has done, and see how close these trades have come to any kind of big announcements in the news. But, since that would only be circumstantial evidence, we're going to need to go further to prove that there's anything illegal."

"No," my dad said. "The illegality ends here. We aren't going to hack him. I won't ask my security firm to do that, even though they can. I think that the best way to approach this would be to find these possibly illegal trades, and *make* Nottingham think that we have definitive proof that he's doing something wrong. If that's what has happened, here. There's no guarantee for that, because, well, Dalilah's information is so vague, it's impossible to know if that's what Nottingham is guilty of."

"Dad," I said. "We need something more definitive. If your security firm can do that, then I think that they should."

Luke gave me a look. I just looked back at him. I felt bad, I did, but I wanted an insurance policy. Simply telling Nottingham that I had information without having something to back it up would be folly, in my opinion.

"No," my dad said. "We aren't going to do that. We're going to find things out legitimately, or not at all."

Nick chimed in. "Ryan, we need to talk about this. We're all involved in this. At least, you and I have our necks on the line, here. I think that we need to take a vote on this. I personally am with Dalilah. I think that we need to get your firm to hack if they have to, to get actual hard information about any kind of illegal trade that he has made. If that's what is going to be our ace, here. There's no guarantee that this is going to be the ace, of course, but who knows what we can find if we really get looking at his hard drive."

My dad was shaking his head. "I hate doing this. I thought that I was out of the illegal stuff a long time ago. I'm getting pulled back into it, though, and I don't like it."

"I know you don't like it, Ryan," Nick said. "But Dalilah is right. We need an insurance policy here."

Dad looked at my mom. "What do you think, beautiful? We do illegal acts to cover up our previous illegal act? Or we try to do things legitimately and let the chips fall where they may?"

My mom sighed. "Ryan, as much as I think that we should do things legally, I know that your security firm is trained in this sort of thing. They're pros. Let them do what they're going to do, and, this way, if Nottingham calls our bluff, we have something concrete to show him."

My dad looked defeated. "Okay, let's take a vote. We're all in this."

"I'm not going to vote, of course," Luke said. "I mean, I don't have a dog in this fight, really. Except, of course, the fact that it's my child who is at the middle of all of this."

"Then you have a dog in the fight," my dad said. "You get a vote, too."

I groaned, inwardly. I knew how Luke was going to vote. I mean, I wasn't certain, but I had a feeling that he was going to vote for doing things dad's way. So, for doing things dad's way, there was Luke and my dad. My mom seemed to be on the side of doing things the hacking way, and Nick did, too. I was clearly on Nick and mom's side.

Which left Scotty. I assumed that she would vote with Nick, but, who knows? Perhaps she, too, was afraid of things going awry if we did things the hacking way.

We took a vote. To my utter surprise, my dad was the only one who voted to not hack. Everyone else, including Luke, voted to have the security firm hack if they had to.

"Okay," Ryan said. "I'm clearly outvoted, here. Now, you all know the risks. Nottingham isn't going to be easy to hack, and, if he finds out he is being hacked, he's going to throw the book at all of us. But, I understand the reason why you guys voted in the way that you did. We do need an insurance policy, and there's more of a chance that this whole thing will go south if there isn't an insurance policy than if there is. So, then, okay. I'm going to have my security firm do whatever it takes to prove that Nottingham has dirty hands."

We spent the rest of the evening planning it all out.

· · ·

That night, after everyone had left, Luke and I spent some time cleaning up the kitchen. We worked in silence for awhile, but I finally brought up the inevitable subject.

"You voted with Nick and everyone against my dad. While I love you for doing that, I was wondering why you would? You were always adamant that I shouldn't do that."

Luke sighed. "Dalilah, I'm trying very hard to reconcile that vote with my own conscience. I'm telling myself that it's different the way that your dad wants to do it, because it's not you doing the hacking. It's the security firm. That's not a great distinction, but that's the one that I'm telling myself."

I nodded. "Well, that sounds like a good distinction to me."

"It's not. Illegal is illegal is illegal. But, at the same time, I agree with Nick and everyone that we're going to have to have insurance with that man. I just don't think that bluffing is going to do it. He's too intelligent. Too devious. I just think that we have to fight fire with fire."

"I love you, you know that? You surprise me sometimes, but in the best way."

"Don't love me for this," Luke said. "This is my dirty side. The side that I don't like. It was bad enough that I had to go into that fetish club with Serena, using a fake badge, but, this...this is just wrong. I wish that there was something else that can be done, and, up until the point where Nottingham started blackmailing you, I really believed it was just going to be two lawyers going at it. To tell you the truth, I think that the fact that he's getting down in the mud is what tipped me over. You can't bring a knife to a gun fight, as you said before."

I held my breath. He clearly was still angry with me.

*Give him time. He'll come around.*

After we did the dishes and cleaned everything up, we sat on the couch together. I rubbed my foot on his crotch playfully, but he gently pushed it away. "I'm sorry, Dalilah, but I'm not in the mood right now."

I felt rebuffed, but tried not to show my hurt.

Then he rubbed my foot, and tried to smile. "Too much stress. Let's go to bed. I somehow have to try to concentrate on getting my art career off the ground, so that I can at least realize a return on my investment. I don't know how I can possibly concentrate on that, though, with all of this nonsense hanging over our heads."

I took a deep breath. "Luke?" I said in a small voice.

"Yes, Dalilah?"

"I made the right decision, right? I mean, in taking the progesterone so that we could keep Olivia?"

Luke looked startled. "Oh, honey, why would you even ask that? Of course you did. That was the only decision to make. That was the best decision you made." Then he shook his head. "But those other decisions. I just don't know. I mean, I know that it all was done for me. But there had to be a better way of going about it. There just had to be."

"20/20 hindsight," I said. "Looking back, I think that I made some of the dumbest decisions imaginable. But, at the time, I thought that these decisions were good. I guess I really wasn't thinking about how underhanded Nottingham was going to turn out to be."

Luke kissed my forehead gently. "So intelligent, yet so naïve at the same time. In a way, a weird way, this makes me actually love you more. You don't always see how dirty people are. I mean, you knew that Nottingham was dirty, but you didn't know how much. I love that you still seem to have a part of you that's optimistic about human nature, no matter what happens."

I sighed with relief. So far, Luke and I were hanging together.

We might have been hanging by a thread, but, as long as we still had even that thread between us, there was a chance that we could get through this.

# Chapter Twenty-Two

## LUKE

I went back to my new studio the day after the big pow-wow that we had with Dalilah's mom, dad, Nick and Scotty. Although I had that whole mess hanging over my head, I had to put my nose to the grindstone. Dalilah brought it home to me when she said that a judge was going to decide the best interest of the child according to income – my income relative to Nottingham's. While I had the feeling it wasn't even going to come to that – who won this battle would be whomever decided to blink first – on the off-chance that this whole mess *would* be decided by a judge, I felt that I had to get my ass in gear.

And, even if the whole mess didn't, in fact, get decided by a judge, I still wanted to get going. Because, no matter what happened, there was going to be a baby in about six more months. In six months, I would be a dad. And I had to provide not only for Dalilah, but also for Olivia. Olivia would be the baby's name, assuming that the baby was a she – Dalilah was scheduled the following week to go in for her first sonogram that would be able to tell the sex of the baby.

For my part, I really hoped that the baby was a girl, for no other reason than the fact that I would have loved to honor my mother with my daughter's name. Of course, I would be happy either way, really.

I was feeling the pressure, for sure. I was still hustling for commissions for myself, and I was also working like hell with the rest of my cooperative in publicizing our upcoming major fund-raiser, which would happen the week after next. So far, the fund-raiser was going to go well, even if it would still be nothing compared to my *Matthew Jane* premiere. We were able to attract attention of a lot of the more minor players in the art world, which was a good thing.

What I wouldn't give, however, for just one of the heavy hitters that attended my premiere to give our cooperative a chance. We would be well on our way if that were the case.

Then, one day that week, the most unexpected thing imaginable happened.

THE DAY STARTED JUST LIKE ANY OTHER. I had gotten into a nice routine of spending about two hours every day composing, about four hours a day helping the cooperative publicize the upcoming fund raiser, and another three hours a day hustling for private commissions. I figured that, since I had a lot of artwork that had, thus far, gone unsold, which meant that I already had a good portfolio, I was better off actually working on the marketing end of my business as opposed to the composing end.

These were long days, but I felt like I was getting somewhere. And that was important, because parting with that initial investment of $20,000 hurt bad. But everybody was cool and hard-working, and there were some massive talents in the cooperative, so I knew that it wouldn't be long until I was making a good income.

The only thing was that I was, essentially, facing a deadline. By the time Olivia came, I felt like I had to have enough money saved up to move out of Serena's home. That was important to me – I had to provide a good home for Dalilah and the baby.

I never even permitted myself to think that Dalilah and I could possibly lose custody to Nottingham. I always assumed that we, as the good guys, were going to win.

My life, aside from worrying and stressing about the entire Nottingham thing, was focused. Laser focused on getting ahead.

So, when I got my unexpected visitor that day, I was shocked. And very pleased.

I was working on a painting when JJ told me that I had somebody there to see me.

"I'll be right there," I said.

"No," JJ said. "I think that you probably shouldn't keep this person waiting."

I rolled my eyes. "I'm right in the middle of something. I'm kinda on a roll."

"Trust me," JJ said. "You want to talk to this person."

Argh! "Okay," I said, following her out. "This better be good."

"It is," she said. "I promise."

I followed her out the lobby of our building, and, standing there, in the flesh, was Henry Jacobs.

I gulped, feeling mixed emotions upon seeing him. I hated him, of course, because he destroyed Dalilah. Yet, I also knew that he was a king-maker, so the mercenary in me was more than happy to see him. I had no idea why he was there, or why he was coming specifically to see me, but I was encouraged that he was there.

"Hello," I said, shaking his hand. "I'm Luke Roberts. I understand that you're here to see me?"

"Yes," Henry said. He was short, about 5'6", balding, with glasses. His posture was slightly hunched. He was very well-dressed, from the shine of his black shoes to the perfectly tailored suit with the little pink handkerchief placed strategically in his jacket pocket. "Mr. Roberts, my name is Henry Jacobs. I'm the lead critic for the *New York Times,* and I was at your premiere back in December. Can we go someplace and talk?"

"Certainly," I said. "Would you like to come back to my studio?"

"I most certainly would," he said. "I'm very interested in your current work. I understand that this cooperative is having a fund-raiser in a few weeks, and I would like for it to be well attended."

I cocked my head, wondering if I was dreaming the entire thing. Henry Jacobs sought me out? After he ignored me in his article about my show, choosing to focus completely on the other two artists who were displaying with me that night? What the hell was going on?

The little man followed me through the maze that led to my studio. Once he got there, he went through my paintings, one by one. He didn't say a word, but I saw him nodding his head several times.

He finally looked at me. "Mr. Roberts, I owe you an apology, so I wanted to deliver it in person. I was at your premiere at the *Matthew Jane*. I found your work exquisite, and I recognized that you were an important artist in the making. But I ignored you in my review of your *Matthew Jane* showing. I would like to rectify that by helping you get the word out about your upcoming fundraiser. I would also like to write a review of your work that you are going to show at your fundraiser. So, please select your most representative paintings for this show."

I was in shock, to be honest. I had no clue that Henry Jacobs even still had me on his radar. "Thank you very much, Mr. Jacobs. I don't know what to say."

He kind of nodded. "You don't have to thank me. I am just trying to correct an injustice. I'll see you at your fundraiser."

And, just like that, he was gone.

I walked out to see JJ, feeling that I was in an absolute daze. "Henry Jacobs is going to be at our fundraiser. And he said that he would like to help get the word out about it."

JJ leaped up in the air. "Whoop!" she said. "Oh my god! Oh my god! Oh.my.god!" She started dancing around the room and shaking her ample hips. "I can't believe it. How did you manage that?"

"Well," I said. "That huge showing I had in December? He didn't write me up, at all. In his review of that show, he completely ignored me. The reason why he came to see me today was that he thought that his ignoring me in that review was an injustice that he wanted to correct. That's probably the craziest thing in the world, huh? I mean, the lead critic for the *New York Times* slumming with us?" I started laughing.

I went to call Dalilah, but then thought better of it. She might not take too kindly to Henry Jacobs being at my fundraiser and publicizing it, considering what he did to her. I finally just decided to tell her when I got home. She might not like it, emotionally, but, rationally, I knew that she would be happy.

It felt like, once again, things might be looking up for me.

But, then again, it felt like that before. I got the rug pulled out from under me that time, and I was afraid that it would happen again. So, I couldn't be overly confident.

I still felt, though, that I had a second chance to make my mark. And I was going to make the most of it.

# Chapter Twenty-Three

I was so stressed out that I was worried about my health, and the health of the baby. My mind was constantly going a mile a minute, trying to anticipate what was about to happen. I felt, however, that I needed something to take my mind off of all of it, so I decided to go down and see Luke at his new studio. I really wanted to get to know the other artists there at the co-op, because I knew that they really wanted me to join them, too. I didn't really have the money for that, however, although I wasn't necessarily above asking my dad to invest in the co-op - if I thought that it would be a good investment.

That was the thing – I needed to know that this cooperative was solid. Then I would know that my father could get a good return for his investment. The last thing that I wanted was for my father just to give me money, without much hope that he would get the money back. Asking him to invest, though, made it seem, to me, like it was another business decision for him, and that made asking him for money all the more palatable.

But, at the same time, I wasn't on the greatest footing with my dad. The reason for this was that, although he wasn't saying as much, I knew that he was pretty pissed at me for the mess I got everybody in. It wasn't the time, just yet, to ask him for the $20,000 investment that I would need to buy into the co-op, considering how tense everything was.

Still, I wanted to get down there and check everything out.

So, imagine my surprise when I went to the co-op and saw Henry Jacobs leaving the premises. I ducked my head, hoping that he wouldn't recognize me. Why I felt the need to hide, I didn't know. I only knew that I felt the need to disguise who I was.

It didn't work.

"Ms. Gallagher?" the little man said to me.

"Hello, Mr. Jacobs," I said. I felt my face flushing red, and I put my hand up to my cheek involuntarily.

"It's good to see you. You're looking well."

I bit my lip and looked down at the floor. While I was surprised to see him, I also felt hopeful yet angry at the same time. Hopeful because I thought that maybe he was there to see Luke, for whatever reason. Angry because I still blamed him for my artistic breakdown. All those years of feeling like a fraud and failure because of him...I couldn't forgive him.

I looked up and he was examining me, as a scientist might examine a subject in an experiment. He had taken off his glasses and was chewing on the end of the frame. He shrugged. "Bad habit."

"Well, it's good to see you too, Mr. Jacobs," I said. "Uh, if you don't mind...." I tried to politely excuse myself, but he apparently didn't get the hint. He still stood there and carefully examined me.

"Ms. Gallagher," he finally said. "I came down here to apologize to Mr. Roberts. Do you know him?"

"Yes, yes I do," I said. This conversation was taking a turn for the surreal, that was for sure.

He took a deep breath. "I think that I might have, as a critic, become a little too immersed in the political side of things. My objectivity has not always been as on-point as it should be. Sometimes there is pressure put upon critics where there really shouldn't be, and people get hurt because of it." Then he paused. "I think that you probably know where I'm going with this."

"I think that I do," I said, although I really didn't. Did he want to print a retraction of his scathing critique, some nine years after the fact? It would be just a little late for that, wouldn't it?

"Ms. Gallagher," he said, "I'm not sure if you have a platform for your work anymore, thanks to me. But if you do, I would be more than happy to review it, wherever it is that you decide to display it." He gave me his card. "Here's my card. Please call me whenever you get a chance to show your work, and I'll guarantee you that I'll write...a more honest review of your work than my previous assessment."

I cocked my head and looked at him quizzically. "Thank you, Mr. Jacobs, but, I confess I don't understand what is motivating this."

"Have you ever had a near-death experience, Ms. Gallagher? Have you ever been at a point in your life when you think that you are going to die, and then you didn't?"

I thought back to when I was a baby. Would that count? It probably would, considering that I was cognizant of what was going on. "Yes, I guess so."

"Well, then, you know what I'm talking about. It changes you, Ms. Gallagher. It makes you realize what's really important in this world, and what isn't." He didn't elaborate further, though. "Well, I'm very glad to have run into you. You wouldn't believe it if I told you this, but you've been on my mind a lot lately. Call it serendipity to run into you this way." He bowed his head a little. "Good day, Ms. Gallagher. I hope to hear from you soon."

At that, he turned on his heel and walked away, his hands in his pocket, and whistling a little tune.

I shook my head. That had to be the oddest thing to happen to me in a long time.

And probably one of the most wonderful things as well.

# Chapter Twenty-Four

## LUKE

I was standing in the lobby with JJ, and she asked me to go to her studio to share a bottle of wine with her. "It's time to celebrate," she said. "Let's call all the other guys in here, too, and tell them the great news."

At that, she called everyone and asked them to meet us in her studio. One by one, everyone showed up, and JJ told them the news.

"Guys," she said. "I'm gathering you all here to tell you that we're going to have a very special guest at our little fund-raiser, and this special guest is going to help us get the word out about it. I predict that this might be a turning point for our little David organization, because Goliath is joining forces with us."

"Really," Arthur, a photographer, said. "Do tell."

"Henry Jacobs will be attending our fund-raiser. And he told Luke here that he's going to help us publicize it. So, everybody, let's make a toast, and then you all have to get to work. Because, just out of the blue, we've gotten the best offer that we ever could hope for, and it seems that this little fund-raiser is going to be better attended then we had ever dreamed."

At that, everybody started chatting excitedly and drinking. "Henry Jacobs, here? I never thought that would happen," said Connie, a sculptor.

"I finally might get somebody to actually care about my work," said Ravi, a painter who specialized in hyper-realism.

I smiled, happy that I could have made this happen. And astounded that it did happen. I never actually thought that anything positive was going to come from that *Matthew Jane* showing, yet it was. It was, and I wasn't the only one who was going to benefit from it.

Then, in the middle of all the celebration, Dalilah walked through the door.

I went over to her and gave her a hug. "Dalilah, you won't believe what just happened."

"Henry Jacobs was here," she said, matter-of-factly.

"How did you know?"

"I ran into him outside. He all but apologized for his unfair critique of my work when I was 11, and told me, in essence, that he was eager to give me a second chance. He said that if I ever got a chance to display my work, he will, quote 'give a more honest review of my work' un-quote."

At that, I picked her up. For just that moment, Nottingham and his threats were forgotten. This was a happy moment for both of us, because we both were getting a second chance to display our work for all to see. And both of us were getting our chance to really get some positive attention, assuming that Henry Jacobs was truly willing to give both of us a positive review.

Dalilah was laughing. "I don't believe this. I mean, it was just a few days ago that I thought that the world was ending. It might still be ending, but today, I just feel happy. I feel happy for you, and for me. We both might get the chance that we never got before."

"Well, now you have something concrete to take to your father if you want him to invest. Tell him that this entire co-op is on its way, if the fund-raiser goes as well as I think it's going to now. Your dad will be more than happy to give you the $20,000, now that he knows that he'll get his investment back."

"Of course, you know that he would be more than willing just to give me that money, even if he wasn't sure if he would get a solid return. It just helps me to know that I'm not asking him to piss in the wind."

"That's one way to put it," I said with a smile. "Well, you and I have work to do. You need to talk to your dad about buying into the co-op, and you need to get your butt in your chair and start painting again. It will take your mind off of what's going on with Nottingham, at least a little bit. Hopefully it will, that is."

At that, Dalilah and I excused ourselves and went into my studio.


DALILAH WENT THROUGH MY PAINTINGS, ONE BY ONE. "There are some that I've never seen before," she said. "Let me help you get the ones together for the fund-raiser."

I went up to her, and lifted up her shirt. She wasn't wearing a bra, and her breasts were swelling more and more by the day. I ran my hand over her burgeoning tummy and stroked it lightly. "God," I said, "you're so sexy these days, I just can't even believe it."

Dalilah turned around and smiled. "Right back atcha, there," she said. And then she turned serious. I could see that he eyes had turned into two pools of lust. Her lips were on mine, hungrily devouring them. I could feel my cock getting harder and harder as she kissed me.

Before long, we were tearing off each other's clothing hungrily. We fell on the couch that I had just brought into the studio, and I was inside her almost immediately. We animalistically merged ourselves on the sofa, until I felt myself spilling my cum into her. Breathless, we both sat up.

"Well, Luke, that was awesome, as always," she said. "But we need to get to work."

Which we did, spending the rest of the day carefully choosing my paintings to show, while listening to music in the background. As we talked and laughed the entire day, it was just like old times. As if there wasn't a Sword of Damocles hanging over our head.

Which it was, of course. There was no denying that. But, for those few hours, it was as if there wasn't a care in the world.


A WEEK WENT BY QUIETLY. Dalilah and I readied ourselves for the other shoe dropping, but it never did. There never was an announcement that the prosecutors were looking into the death of Paul Lucas, although we both held our breaths in waiting for just such an announcement.

In the meantime, we also prepared for the fund-raiser. Dalilah was becoming more active by the day in helping out, and she was close to asking her father for the money for her to be able to join the co-op as well. She hadn't asked him yet, however, because she was worried about the tension that was still between her and Ryan. She knew that he was still angry with her, so she felt intimidated to say anything to him.

We also found out the real reason for Henry Jacobs' change of heart. When Dalilah told me that Henry told her that he had a near-death experience, we decided to find out if there was anything on the news about it. It turned out that there was, but, because we were in London at the time that it happened, we didn't know about it.

So, we Googled it, and the news articles turned up immediately. An intruder had broken into his home and shot him when Henry tried to defend himself with his personal gun. The bullet came very close to nicking his aorta, although it didn't quite, and he had a touch and go surgery. The article indicated that Henry felt that he was lucky to be alive.

I smiled. "So, the old fart has a conscience after all. I wonder if he told Nottingham to stuff it, assuming that Nottingham's pressure was what caused him to ignore me in the first place."

"I'm quite sure that Nottingham's pressure was the reason why Henry ignored you," Dalilah said. "After all, he said something to me about how politics had colored the way that he has critiqued shows, and he wasn't going to let that happen anymore. Well, good for him, being more independent like that. I wonder how the paper feels about him being more independent, though."

I shrugged. "Who knows? It seems that politics plays a part in too many things these days. How naïve of us to ever believe that anybody can be truly objective, when there's always money and pressure involved in everything people do anymore."

"That's very true," she said.

Then, one day, while Dalilah and I were readying ourselves for the big fund-raiser, she got a phone call.

From her father.

The security team had given him their report.

# Chapter Twenty-Five

## DALILAH

My heart was in my throat when I got that phone call from my dad. "Dalilah," my father said on the phone. "We need to talk."

"Okay," I said. "Let's talk."

"Not here," he said. "Let me meet you at a restaurant of your choice there in your neighborhood."

I didn't know if I liked his tone of voice. I prayed that the security firm found something. Something juicy. Something illegal. Something that would give me ammunition and would force Nottingham to back the hell off.

"I'll be there in an hour," I said, after my dad told me that he was in town, so he could be in my neighborhood as soon as possible.

I looked at Luke. "That was my dad. He said that he got the report back from his security firm."

"Let's go," Luke said.

At that, we went down to the restaurant, ordered a whiskey sour for him and soda water for me, and waited for my dad.

He appeared within the hour. He looked happy, and I felt my heart soar. Perhaps things were going to go our way after all.

Luke and I stood up when he arrived in the place, and we all sat down.

"Okay," dad said, "let's get down to business."

I nodded, feeling optimistic yet terrified all at the same time.

"Your hunch was correct," dad said. "Nottingham made several extremely suspicious transactions that coincided with important FDA announcements. Not just one, but around ten. Three of the transactions involved him buying thousands of shares of stocks in pharmaceutical companies just before these companies announced the approval of a new drug. The other seven involved him completely dumping stocks just before the FDA announced negative news about these same companies. In four of these incidents, he dumped stocks for pharmaceutical companies that were involved in class-action lawsuits right after he dumped the stocks. In the other three of these incidents, Nottingham dumped stocks right before product recalls."

I rubbed my hands together. "Oh, this is great. This is awesome! Sounds like we have the smoking gun!"

My dad nodded his head. "It would be pretty difficult for him to explain that all away. Too many incidents for him to say that it was all a coincidence. At any rate, there's enough there to get the SEC sniffing around him pretty hard, and I predict that Nottingham isn't going to want that."

"Okay, then," I said. "Let me set up a meeting with him. Now that I have him dead to right, I predict that he's going to back off of everything."

I CALLED NOTTINGHAM RIGHT AFTER I HAD MY MEETING WITH MY DAD.

"Hello, Blake," I said.

"Dalilah," he said, coolly. "Pleasure to talk to you."

"Oh, no, it's my pleasure," I said. "Shall we meet? I have a few things that I need to talk to you about."

"Seven o'clock," he said. "At Nobu in Tribeca." At that, he hung up.

I rolled my eyes. My father was still sitting there at the lunch table. "Can you get your limo to take me to Nobu tonight at seven?" I asked him.

"I'll get right on it," he said, and then called his driver. "Okay, it's set. Now, how are you going to approach this?"

"I will just tell him that we have evidence that he's been engaging in many acts of insider trading, and that I would put in an anonymous tip to the SEC if he doesn't back off. God knows that the information that we have just might be the tip of the iceberg. Nottingham could be facing some serious prison time for just these transactions. Just think about the possibility of there being even more."

My father sighed. "Yes. Well, I guess we have to live with the morality of this. After all, if he's engaging in high-level fraud, we really should report him. Yet, we're not going to, because we know that if we do, Nottingham is going to turn around and contact the prosecutors about Paul Lucas, and we're all going to be in hot water."

"By the way," I said to my father. I had long since gotten a new phone, but I had given my old phone to the security team to try to debug. "Did they find the bug in my phone – your security team?"

"Yes," my dad said. "It was microscopic, but they found it. Your phone is safe to use if you want, but I know that you're probably still leery about it. If you want, they can destroy it."

"Sure," I said. "I already have all the information off of that phone that I need. Have them destroy it completely. I don't want to take the chance that there might be something else on the phone that they might have missed."

"Will do," dad said.

We talked for a few more hours, and, at some point, I brought up the possibility that he might invest in the co-op by giving me the $20,000 buy-in. "You'll get the money back, dad, and thensome," I said. "With Henry Jacobs supporting Luke and me, we should really be able to make a go of it."

My dad warmed to the idea. "Sounds ideal for you, Dalilah," he said. "It's always been my dream that you would find your way. It sounds like you finally are. You're going to have a baby, and it sounds like you might have found a really good group who will help you with your career. And a solid relationship with a great guy like Luke, here," he said, putting his hand on Luke's shoulder. "Now, if we can just get this pesky

Nottingham situation under control, you might just be on your way, Dalilah."

"Yeah," I said. "A pesky, tiny problem like Nottingham has to be vanquished before I can feel that I'm able to breathe."

That would come later, of course. At that moment, I was savoring my time with my father and Luke.

I ARRIVED AT NOBU RIGHT AT 7. I took several deep breaths as I walked into the restaurant. Nottingham was already there, of course, drinking some hot Saki. "Hello, Dalilah," he said as I arrived at the table. "It's good to see you. I hope that you've been going to your prenatal appointments and doing everything right. Our baby has to have every chance."

"*My* baby is fine, according to my latest prenatal visit," I said. "It's a girl, in fact," I said, and this was true. That was confirmed with a sonogram.

"A little girl," he said. "That's going to be great."

"Okay," I said. "I'm not beating around the bush. I want you to go to your lawyer and sign papers that would terminate any rights that you have to this child. I want you to do this tomorrow."

Nottingham chuckled, but I saw fear in his eyes. I read his eyes well – he knew that I knew. But he was still going to try to bluff.

"I'll do no such thing," he said. "I was going to ask you to drop your contesting of my rightful paternity of this child."

"Okay," I said. "I'll do that, but, before I do, I think that I might make a phone call to the SEC. An anonymous phone call that will indicate that you, Blake Nottingham, have been engaging in a pattern of insider trading. And, while they're at it, I'm quite sure that they will be looking for every other evidence of the fraud that I'm quite sure that you're engaging in."

"Insider trading?" Nottingham said. "I have no idea what you're talking about."

"I'm talking about ten different incidents where you either bought stock right before the FDA announced the approval of a new drug or dumped stock right before bad news hit. Now, don't try to bullshit me,

Blake. I have evidence that you did this, and, as you know, an anonymous tip is all that is necessary to get the SEC sniffing around you like Duke the bloodhound on the *Beverly Hillbillies*. And don't think that you're too rich to go to prison – if Bernie Madoff and Martha Stewart weren't too wealthy to go to prison, then you won't be either."

Nottingham narrowed his eyes. I could see hatred in those eyes, and, as he took a sip of his Saki, I thought that he would come across the table and strangle me with his bare hands.

Finally he said, "okay. I'll have my attorney draw up papers tomorrow that will terminate my rights to your little brat. But know this. If I ever find out that you went ahead and called the SEC, I'll be down at the prosecutors office immediately, and your father and Nick will be in prison in no time. What they did was even worse than what you're accusing me of. Fair warning."

I nodded my head, my heart soaring. "Goes without saying, Blake. Don't worry, your secret is safe with me."

At that, I got up. "I'm not hungry. Besides, I'm not supposed to eat sushi. I'll call my attorney tomorrow. If there are not papers filed by your attorney by the end of the day tomorrow, I'll be calling the SEC."

He snorted. "It would be just like you to throw your dad and Nick under the bus like that, wouldn't it? To call the SEC, even though you know what will happen if you do?"

"Do you want to take that chance?" I asked.

"No," he said. "It's not worth it. Have a nice life, Dalilah."

I walked out of the restaurant, relieved.

He blinked first.

Hopefully.


THE NEXT DAY, I WAITED, with bated breath, for the news that Nottingham's attorney filed the necessary papers. Truth be told, I was scared. I didn't know if Nottingham would take the chance that I wouldn't go through with calling the SEC, even if he continued to force the paternity issue, just because there was no way that I would take the chance that Nottingham would go the prosecutor's office.

He probably knew that. Would he go back on his word?

I paced around Luke's studio all that day.

"Sit down, Dalilah," Luke said. "You're making me nervous. It's going to be okay. Nottingham won't take the chance that he's going to go to prison. He has to know that, between you and him, you have more reason to bring him down then he does you. You have more at stake, therefore, he's going to calculate that you're going to be more willing than him to do all you can to fight."

"I know that," I said. "I'm looking at it the same way. But if he calls my bluff, and still fights me, what do I do? I have this information on him, but what good does it do if it ends up with my dad and Nick being prosecuted?"

"Dalilah," Luke said. "If Nottingham thinks that there is even a slight chance that you could bring him down, he'll do what you want. So, relax."

At that, he brought me down on his lap, and raised my hair up so that he could kiss my neck. "Mmmmm," he said, rubbing my belly. "It won't be long until I can feel Olivia start kicking."

I turned around, and kissed him. He breathed in deep, his cock getting hard. He rubbed my back, under my shirt, and kissed me passionately.

As I started to lift up his shirt, though, the phone rang.

It was my attorney.

"Hello," I said, eagerly.

"Dalilah?" Marissa said. "I'm glad that I caught you."

"Yes," I said. "Do you have news for me?"

"I do," she said. "Good news. Nottingham's attorney has filed a motion with the court to ask the court to terminate his rights to the unborn child. Congratulations!"

I screamed when she told me that. "Luke, Luke, Luke!" I said. "He did it! He filed the papers!"

Luke started laughing, and he picked me up.

"Oh, I'm so sorry, Marissa, I just told my boyfriend about this. He and I are over the moon now!"

She laughed. "Well, this certainly has made this case easier. Now it's just a matter of property division."

"No," I said. "I don't want any property from him. I just want this done. Please put this on the uncontested docket, and we'll get this over with."

"You got it," she said. "I'll call you back with the date."

I hung up, and Luke and I started dancing around the room. "Oh, my god, Luke, our long nightmare is almost over. I just can't believe it. I just can't believe it."

He kissed me. "Believe it," he said. "Our long nightmare might be coming to an end, but our dream is just beginning."

It was. Our dream was just beginning.

# Chapter Twenty-Six

## ONE WEEK LATER

"Okay, Luke," I said. "It's show time."

He smiled. "Show time part *deux*, huh? Let's hope that this show has a longer lasting impact than the last one did."

"It will," I said, walking around the little gallery that was owned by the co-op. The Thiessen Gallery, according to Henry Jacobs in his latest column, was one to watch. He wrote a glowing profile of all the artists in the co-op prior to the show, and the tickets to the fund-raiser were sold out.

JJ said that was the first time that they had ever sold all the tickets. "It's going to be an excellent show," she said.

Of course it was going to be. There were going to be hundreds of people there, from hipsters to businessmen who were interested in commissioning some hot new artists. Because the tickets were all sold, the co-op was able to invest in a better menu, better alcohol and better live entertainment.

It was going to be fun night.

AND IT WAS A FUN NIGHT. A very fun night. It was more relaxed than the *Matthew Jane* affair, and a little more boisterous. The co-op hired a small jazz band to play music, and the alcohol and hors d'oeuvres were consumed freely. I even saw Henry Jacobs smile and laugh as he made his way around the crowd.

"Looks like it's a hit," I said to Luke, taking his arm. I was happy, very happy, because Nottingham and I had just finalized our divorce several days prior. I was a single woman, again, and I hoped that Luke and I would soon be engaged once more.

"I hope that it is," he said. "I have to provide for that little baby there, so it would certainly be helpful if my art career can finally achieve lift-off."

"Not to mention my career," I said. My father gave me the money to buy into the co-op, and I was going to be moving into my own studio within a matter of days.

"Oh, I'm not worried about that," he said. "You're awesome. You're going to be on top in no time at all."

I laughed. "We'll see, Luke. We'll see."

And, at that, I felt, for the very first time, Olivia kick. I put my hand on my stomach, and tears came to my eyes.

"What is it, Dalilah?" Luke asked, looking concerned.

I shook my head. "Olivia. She just kicked." I started laughing. "Here, feel."

He did, putting his hand on my stomach. He felt it, and he started laughing, too. "Wow," he said. "That's amazing." He continued to feel, as Olivia kicked several more times. "Are we sure that's a girl? It feels like some kind of NFL kicker in there."

"Hey," I said. "Maybe when Olivia is older, she'll be able to play in the NFL. You never know."

Luke laughed. "True that," he said. "True that."

ALL IN ALL, THE SHOW WAS AN OVERWHELMING HIT. Every artist sold at least three paintings, and the revenue from the party was enough that the co-op, as a whole, made a nice profit off of the evening. Luke actually sold five of his paintings at $5,000 apiece, so he was more than happy to have at least made back his initial investment in the co-op.

But what really was the icing on the cake was the review that Henry Jacobs wrote about the evening. He focused on Luke's work, and he wrote about it in glowing terms. Henry concluded that Luke was *the* artist to watch, and he predicted a bright future.

And, in the coming weeks, that prophecy finally started to come true. After the show, and Henry Jacobs' review, Luke was finally in demand. People were lining up to give him commissioned work, and, suddenly, Luke's income was more than either of us could have ever dreamed.

"We can finally get a place of our own," Luke had said. We were still staying at Serena's, because she was okay with us being there until we could actually find a better place. Which meant that I chose not to go back to my old apartment, and the sub-lessor was able to stay. My old place was way too small for the three of us, so Luke was hoping that he could afford a larger place, perhaps a brownstone of his own in the same neighborhood as Serena.

I would have thought that was a pipe dream, but Luke's commissions were truly astounding. The first client who hired him offered him $50,000 for a commissioned painting, and everyone else who lined up behind this client offered Luke the same or even more. Luke had the aura of an up and coming artist, thanks to Henry Jacobs, and he was very much in demand.

I had to laugh at the irony of it all. Henry Jacobs, the same guy who destroyed me, ended up being our savior. And I knew that, once I started heavily producing, he would be on my side as well. And Nottingham, my ultimate nemesis, was still responsible for Luke's great career. Because, without that *Matthew Jane* showing, Henry Jacobs never would have known about Luke.

It was crazy how things work out sometimes.

Turns out that my machinations were fruitful after all.